Follow THE KID as he and the Dodgers battle for the top in WORLD SERIES. Then watch as THE KID COMES BACK an injured, war-torn veteran returning to stardom despite the threat of becoming a lifelong cripple.

THE KID FROM TOMKINSVILLE,
WORLD SERIES,
THE KID COMES BACK,
novels about the most exciting baseball hero of all time by JOHN R. TUNIS, the dean of sports fiction writing.

THE KID FROM TOMKINSVILLE

by John R. Tunis

Illustrated by Jay Hyde Barnum

BANTAM BOOKS
TORONTO NEW YORK LONDON

This low-priced Bantam Book
has been completely reset in type face
designed for easy reading, and was printed
from new plates. It contains the complete
text of the original hard-cover edition.
NOT ONE WORD HAS BEEN OMITTED.

RLI: VLM 5 (VLR 4–6)
IL 4+

THE KID FROM TOMKINSVILLE
A Bantam Book / published by arrangement with
Harcourt Brace Jovanovich, Inc.

PRINTING HISTORY
Harcourt Brace Jovanovich edition published March 1940
Bantam edition / April 1977

ISBN 0–553–02271–7

Published simultaneously in the United States and Canada

Bantam Books are published by Bantam Books, Inc. Its trademark, consisting of the words "Bantam Books" and the portrayal of a bantam, is registered in the United States Patent Office and in other countries, Marca Registrada. Bantam Books, Inc., 666 Fifth Avenue, New York, New York 10019.

PRINTED IN THE UNITED STATES OF AMERICA

The author wishes to state
that all the characters in this book
were drawn from real life.

Illustrations

THE KID FROM TOMKINSVILLE

1

The train stood still. The train seemed attached to the station forever. The train refused to leave. So did his friends. They balanced first on one foot and then on the other along the platform below his window, the girls giggling, the boys grinning and shouting things it was impossible to hear. Embarrassed and unhappy, he slouched down in the seat. They were attracting attention and people ahead in the car turned to stare, looking at his one small suitcase with the bat strapped to it in the rack above. Their staring increased his loneliness and his fear of going away into the unknown, the fear of leaving home for the first time which suddenly took possession of him. If only the train would leave. But the train didn't move.

The door just behind him banged and a brakeman came through. The last words of the conductor standing beside the steps with his watch in hand filtered through the door before it shut.

"Yeah . . . that kid from Tomkinsville . . ." The brakeman turned and looked at him curiously as he passed down the aisle. Other passengers caught the words and turned to look also. Still the train refused to move. Then there was a jolt. It did move. Slowly, gently, but it moved. Instantly the group below became animated and started to wave. He straightened up and waved back. They followed the car along the platform; boys he had played and fought with, girls with whom he'd gone to school: Joe and Harry Cousins, the twins who played end on the football team; Harry Peters, whose father had also been killed in the war; Jess Moore and Tommy Watson, who had the night shift at MacKenzie's drugstore, and Jim Harrison, who was taking his place on the day shift, and . . . and lots of others, now disappearing. Only a minute before he had wished them all a million miles away. Now they were his last link with Grandma and Tomkinsville. He couldn't bear to see them vanish so he turned and waved. Then the train gathered speed and they were out of sight. He was alone. . . .

The door opened brusquely and the conductor came in accompanied by a draft of cold air. "Tickets, please, Hartford tickets. . . ." Reaching into his pocket, he noticed the conductor was smiling. That ticket . . . where was it? His pocketbook, his inside pocket . . . but he had it . . . only half an hour before. A panic seized him. Lost? Ah, there it was. In a side pocket where he had stuffed it as he shook hands with them on the platform. He handed it to the conductor and as he did so a copy of *Detective Stories*, his reading material for twenty-four hours, fell to the floor. The conductor casually unfolded the long green strip, punched it several times, and handed it back. "Clearwater, hey . . . going down to the training camps?" Then he went up the aisle.

"Tickets . . . Hartford tickets, please."

Folks up ahead in the car turned and stared.

. . . .

The knot of men round the train gate of the Pennsylvania Station suddenly came alive as the uniformed attendant dropped the chain and called out:

"Palmetto Limited; Jacksonville, Tampa, St. Petersburg, Sarasota, and the West Coast. Palmetto Limited." Beside him a tall man in a fawn-colored coat with a piece of paper in his hand was checking the men as they went through the gate. He called out each name. "Cars 456 and 7, boys. Townsend . . . Loretti . . . Spencer . . . Brooks . . . yeah, you're in 456 . . . Henricks . . . Stevens . . . Smith . . . Case, where's Case? . . . there you are . . . Scudder . . . I got you, Scudder . . . Hennessey . . . Bareto . . . Morgan . . . Rice . . . 456 and 7 . . ."

While the crowd surged about the narrow entrance, a well-dressed man at one side stood watching and waiting for the gate to clear. Two porters behind him were surrounded by a mountain of luggage; expensive leather handbags, large suitcases, and an enormous bag crammed with several dozen clubs and bulging with golf paraphernalia. At his elbow was a short, chunky, red-faced fellow with his gray hat over his eyes and his hands in the pockets of his trousers. The older man was talking and shaking his head with decision.

"No . . . of course I won't say that. . . . How can I? Haven't seen the other clubs yet." There was some annoyance in his voice. "Nope, I certainly won't say that, Casey. Don't know yet." He flipped away his cigarette with a derisive gesture. Then he turned to the porters, nodded, and followed by that mountain of baggage moved toward the train gate. The smaller man kept close beside him, and they passed through and descended the stairs to the waiting train. "What's that? . . . Well, I dunno. . . . Maybe . . . Maybe not . . . How can I tell? . . . Sure, you can say that. You can say we won't finish last like we did last summer. What's that? New men? Well . . . coupla swell outfielders from the Pacific Coast League, and a fair shortstop who hit .320 for Elmira last season, and a boy named Stevens from Kansas City who won eighteen games for 'em, and . . . oh, yes, there's a kid from Connecticut, they tell me he'll be a ballplayer in a few years. Car 517." The Pullman conductor at the foot of the stairs waved him up ahead. "My car's in front. C'mon up and have dinner. All I know is I have a hundred and fifty grand invested in that ballclub. I'll say this. We got problems. Plenty of problems. But if we can come up with two good pitchers we'll make any of 'em hustle." He turned abruptly and went forward. The two porters followed him into the blackness.

The little man went into his car. As the train started he unhitched a portable typewriter, set it up, inserted a piece of paper and began to write. Then he hesitated. He took the paper out and threw it away in a crumpled ball. He put in another sheet and after a few words repeated the process. All this time the train was rocking across the meadows of Newark. Once again he tried it, once more he was dissatisfied, took the paper out and tossed it aside. As they slowed up at the station in Newark he lit a cigarette, leaned back and smoked. Finally he put in a fresh sheet and wrote at the top of the page:

"BY JIM CASEY

"Unless it's an old man selling apples at the corner of Broad and Chestnut streets, Philadelphia, on a cold winter day, I can't think of anything more pathetic than setting out with the Brooklyn Dodgers for another season." His cigarette was out so he lit another and continued. The words came faster. "Who've they got this year? For pitchers, Jake Kennedy, Frenchie De Voe, Harry Norman, Rats Doyle, Sam Henderson, 'Fat Stuff' Foster and Razzle Nugent. Except for Nugent Foster is the best of a bad lot. He had the best record last summer when he lost twenty games and won ten. That means the Dodgers are exactly half a game behind every time he takes the mound. They have a rookie from Elmira trying for shortstop, two new outfielders from the Pacific Coast, and a kid from somewhere up in Connecticut without any big-league experience who's supposed to pitch them into the Series. Maybe."

Now words rippled from his machine. His face grew redder, for he was thinking of the effect of those sentences on the man in the car up front. After all, what of it? True, every word. He read what he had written and as the spires of Princeton whizzed past in the distance he inserted a final sheet and ended his story.

"If you think all this is hard on our Dodgers, just do one thing. Clip this and call me on it next September. Then if the Dodgers aren't in last place, sue me. No, don't sue me. Choke me, because I have no business being a sportswriter."

• • • • • • •

"Drive?"

He shook his head as he shoved the third suitcase into the back of the car. "Nope. You drive." She got in behind the wheel and he opened the other door and sat down. Anything to postpone the time when responsibility for the family would be on his shoulders.

She took the wheel, backed out of the driveway and drove down the familiar street. The children waved to him from the front window and he waved back. A flurry of snow beat against the glass, and he leaned over to turn on the car heater. At the corner a commuter coming home from work with his head lowered against the storm seemed weary and beaten. The man in the car watched the snow fall. The same sort of storm as the day he had started for the training camps the first time, a boy fresh from college going into the big leagues. He remembered the bitter cold, the driving snow, and then the warmth and sunshine of Florida the next day. Those were the days when roughnecks ruled the training camps, when you could turn in at night and be sure of finding a dead shark in your bed. Things were different now, and easier. If only he was breaking in nowadays.

They turned into Wayne Avenue, past the A & P, and then by Johnson's drugstore where the boys always listened to the out-of-town games on the air—or said they did. The car swung into Germantown as she stopped for a red light. "I'm sure things won't be as bad as you imagine, Dave. Look how well you feel. You haven't had a cold this winter. You're young still. . . ."

"I know I'm young. You know I'm young. I feel young all right. But does he know it? You can't fool the record book. After all, there it is. Started in 1923 with the Chicago White Sox. Laugh that one off. The oldest catcher in the big leagues. That's what the papers always say. Notice, not the smartest catcher, or the best catcher, but the oldest catcher. The veteran . . ."

"Dave Leonard! Stop! You *are* the smartest catcher. Casey said so. With all your experience you have something to offer them, especially a young club that must be built up from the bottom." He shook his head. She was encouraging him or at least she was trying to encourage him, to help, but he knew she was merely repeating words. They helped yet they hurt.

"Casey! What's he know about baseball? Well, anyway . . . there's one sure thing. They don't pay twelve-five for nothing these days. I know I'm not as young as Stansworth. Stansworth can catch a hundred and fifty games . . . I . . . can catch a hundred, though . . . easily." There was a tone of eagerness in his voice. "Stansworth's young. But they don't pay him twelve-five. Yet, anyhow."

Ah, if he was only twenty-seven and breaking into the League again with all the things he knew. With the things you get only through experience, through watching carefully and studying each man and each style of play, through making mistakes, errors that cost games, that cost a lead, that cost a team the pennant, that cost twenty-five players their share in the World Series gate. That's when you learn. He'd learned.

But he was thirty-eight. Dave Leonard the veteran, you know, fella used to catch for the White Sox. Oldest catcher in the game now. Her hand came over his as she read his thoughts. Then she reached for the gear because a red light showed ahead.

Twelve-five. They don't pay salaries like that to rookie catchers at any rate. Nor to veterans either, for long. The house back on Elliott Avenue, and those kids at the window, the three people who depended on that twelve-five, what would they do when his contract wasn't renewed? Thirty-eight. In baseball it was speed that counted, and at thirty-eight your speed was gone. At thirty-eight the average business man is just getting into the money. In baseball a chap is just leaving it. Twelve-five, yep, sounds like lots of money. But he needed three years before some of his insurance came due and the load lightened.

The station loomed ahead, and she turned and swung inside. The car bumped as they went up the drive.

"Needs new springs," she said, half apologetically.

"Needs a new car," he answered bitterly. She stopped and a porter opened the door.

"Yeah . . . those three small bags. Palmetto Limited." She got out and went into the station with him. Someone going past reached for his arm. "Hi, there, Dave old boy, going South? Good luck to you." He smiled, shook hands, and hurried on.

"Who was that, Dave?"

"Dunno. Some man, some fan I guess. Maybe the guy who threw the bottle at me when I struck out in that game last fall." Whoever the man was he had a job, a real job, not just a job for the summer. Not a veteran ballplayer, finished and ready to be shoved off at thirty-eight. Thirty-eight, and then who knows; perhaps his last year in the League. After that what? Kansas City, or Beaumont, or Nashville, tank towns with half salary for a few years, and then back for a job on the coaching lines like old Gallagher who'd once caught Alexander and now hardly made enough to keep through the winter.

"Now . . . now . . . what's that you're saying?" Yes, he must be getting old, muttering to himself. They went along the platform hand in hand, he holding her and reluctant to let her go. "Remember, dear, this isn't your last season. I know it isn't. With your experience you won't be just a bullpen catcher. How do you know, maybe you'll get a job as manager. Just you wait and see."

He shook his head. Managers' jobs didn't come just for the asking. Then a loudspeaker bellowed a warning. "Stand back, please. Palmetto Limited; Jacksonville, Tampa, St. Pete, Sarasota and the West Coast." Still pressing her close he walked ahead as the train with a roar from behind rumbled past, slithered down to a hissing stop. He glanced up at the lighted cars and saw a face he knew. Another, and another. Red Allen, the first baseman. Casey, the sportswriter, his hands in his pockets as usual, standing on the platform with a cigarette in his mouth. And someone . . . someone who waved at him he didn't recognize. Those familiar faces cheered him.

"Yo' car up ahead, boss. 456. Up ahead." They went up hand in hand. Those faces helped, friends who liked him and would be in there fighting in the dead heat of St. Louis and Cincinnati in July, fellows who knew what it was to stick through a losing game with a losing team. Easy enough to have pepper when you were in second place. But when you were last; that's when it was hard to fight.

Car 456. Here it was. "Tampa, Clearwater, St. Pete, Sarasota next car."

"Good-by, Helen."

"Good-by. Don't worry. Things will work out; you'll see. Take care of yourself at first. Don't overdo."

He climbed up, turned and waved to her, and went inside. The bright lights of the interior dazzled him momentarily, but the sound of familiar voices calling his name greeted his ears.

"There he is now. . . ."

"Hey, Dave, old boy. . . ."

"How's the old kid, Dave, how arya? . . ."

. . . .

"What's the sign say?"

"Sez Tampa, 22 miles."

"Suits me. This driving gets tiresome. Never driven down before and I won't drive down again." The big Cadillac was leaping down a straight road bordered on one side by the railroad track and on the other by pine groves. It was a brand-new car glistening in the afternoon sunshine, driven with sureness and touch by the blond man at the wheel. He must have driven expensive cars all his life, for there was an air of authority in his grasp of the wheel which seemed to go with cars like Cadillacs.

"Saw Murphy last night in the lobby."

"Bill Murphy? Giants' manager?"

"Yeah."

"What's he doing up there?"

"On a scouting trip."

"What's he say?"

"Says the Yanks are hot this year. Says he seen you with your arms round MacManus' neck in a picture. Guesses that'll be the last time it'll be there unless you grab off a pennant."

"Wait till Mac hears that one. It'll burn him up. Funny about those two guys, they sure get in each other's hair, don't they? Mac's been okay with me. He's tough, so is a good ballplayer."

"Yeah . . . well, I ain't noticed you were very easy pickings. You always looked out for yourself pretty good."

"Who else? No one ever helped me into the big leagues. I fought my own way up, ever since I was a kid I fought, ever since I was a kid with no money to buy shoes in Montpelier, Vermont."

"Yeah. You're a scrapper all right. That Gas

House Gang, they're all scrappers. They sure weren't a bunch of sissies. Great gang, those boys."

"Scrapping wins pennants. I'd like this team to be scrappers. To be a hustling ballclub, no lead in their tails. We got too many nice boys. Too much dead wood. Old Caswell and Jennison and Dave Leonard. Been in the League almost twenty years, he has. I want youngsters. Like this-here-now Kid from Tomkinsville. They tell me he'll be a ballplayer one of these days . . . maybe. . . ." He added the last word as an afterthought. When you've been up and around a few years in baseball and seen a few of them come and go, when you've watched kids with big reputations in the minors go to pieces for no reason at all with a big-league club, well, you get sort of cautious.

• • • • • • •

In the coach behind the baggage car in front of the train, the Kid from Tomkinsville stretched his legs for the twentieth time in an hour. The dog-eared and dirty copy of *Detective Stories* fell to the ground and stayed there because he had read it through, some stories twice over. He ached everywhere. Sleeping in a day coach does things to you. No matter how you sit or what position you take, you wake up sore and weary. Your neck is stiff. The jolting and rocking of the train tightens your leg muscles. It makes your hips and thighs ache. The thick, unchanged air contracts your throat and gives you a heavy feeling in your head, the continual dust irritates your nasal passages. Outside the warm afternoon sunshine beat through dingy window panes into the stuffy interior of the car. They had left Washington the previous night in a blizzard, but the sun was shining at Jacksonville in the morning. It was a pleasant, warm, and welcome sun. Now it was hot and much less welcome. A long flat road wound beside the track with groves of pine trees beyond. Slowly a big blue car came into sight, and he envied the two bareheaded men sitting in the front. It was an expensive cabriolet with the top back, and suitcases and golf bags piled high in the rear. A couple of millionaires, probably, going South for a winter vacation. Some folks had all the luck. Now the car swerved close to the train, then it veered away as the road shifted, but always it moved gently ahead until finally it pulled out of sight.

Some day he'd have a car like that. A big shiny, blue-painted car, and take Grandma for a ride in it with the top back. Some day, when he was a successful ballplayer.

2

Funny how a chap can feel lonely even in a crowd.

The crowd made him feel more lonely than ever. Because those men in the roof garden at breakfast didn't seem like ballplayers, not at least the kind he knew, but older men. They were business men, well-dressed fellows who were evidently prospering in a profession that they liked. They wore curious costumes—coats that didn't match their gray trousers and pointed tan shoes with white tips. Everyone seemed to know everyone else; they called each other by their first names, and jokes and laughter floated across the tables as they looked at the menu with practiced glances, ordered what they wanted, and addressed the waitress as "Sweetmeat." It made him feel terribly alone. He sat at a table unoccupied save for his roommate, a boy with big open brown eyes who like himself sat in silence, knowing no one.

Down in the lobby after breakfast it was worse. While he sat silently in a big chair, men kept coming downstairs, greeting old friends, calling in delight as they found a pal, laughing and talking, perfectly at ease, with no worries or fears. He was not only unhappy, he was afraid, and his loneliness accentuated his fright. There was the fear of not making good, of having to return home without a job as everyone in Tomkinsville had predicted. Worst of all, there was the worry as to whether he'd ever be able to return. Suppose he couldn't make the grade? Lots of rookies didn't. Suppose . . . Then a man stalked across the lobby in front of his chair.

The man was tall, broad-shouldered, quietly but expensively dressed in blue striped trousers, a blue sports coat, and the whitest of white sports shoes. The ballplayers all had tan shoes with white tips, but his shoes were white all over. There was something impressive in the way he walked, or maybe in the way he swayed his shoulders, and the gesture with which he twirled his Panama in his hand as he moved over to the newsstand. He picked up a newspaper with decisive movement. One . . . two . . . three . . . four . . . now what does anyone want five newspapers for? There was even decision in the way he folded them and snapped them under his arm, turned and walked down the stairs to the street. This man was somebody. Someone who'd done things. He was sure of himself. He was . . .

Of course. It was MacManus.

Jack MacManus, the man who broke into the big leagues straight from Minnesota, the guy who enlisted as a private in the war and came out a colonel, who went back to college and played on a Big Ten championship football team, who started off in the big leagues by spiking Ty

Cobb when Ty tried to run him down as a fresh young busher. Man who'd made a million dollars in oil, lost it in the market, re-made it in radio, bought a minor league club, and finally picked up the Dodgers the year before. The Kid knew about MacManus. Everyone in baseball knew about him. Chap who put Columbus on the map, who started night baseball, who was forever scrapping with someone: Judge Landis, the umpires, or Bill Murphy; yes, his feud with the Giant manager was famous. That was MacManus all right. It couldn't be anyone else. No wonder he walked that way, held himself like that. He resembled Mr. Haskins, the president of the First National Bank at home, who got the Kid his job in MacKenzie's drugstore on the corner of South Main. All at once the difference became apparent. This man was the real thing. Mr. Haskins was small town and small time. An idol tumbled as those broad shoulders sauntered down the steps of the Fort Harrison Hotel into the deep Florida sun.

If that was MacManus, and it couldn't be anyone else, why not settle things immediately? A resolution seized the Kid. Beneath the porch, papers under his arm, his feet wide apart, the great man stood, regarding the sunny street through his dark glasses, and waiting for his car. Without further thought or considering what he was doing, or how he would be received, the Kid darted down the steps.

"Mr. MacManus . . . I'm . . . I'm Roy Tucker. . . ."

He started and turned round. There was half a frown on his face, but the freckles on his nose were reassuring and through the dark glasses his eyes were blue and crinkly round the corners. He looked up quickly. "Who . . . oh, yeah . . . Roy Tucker . . . sure, the Kid from Tomkinsville . . . yeah, mighty glad to see you, fine to have you with us." He held out a hand. It was a lean, strong hand and the grip was encouraging.

"Why, sure, I remember the afternoon you pitched against those Cuban All-Stars in Waterbury last summer. Hope you'll show us something like that down here."

"Uhuh. I sure hope. That's what I wanted to ask. Mr. MacManus. If you . . . if the team . . . in case you can't use me at all, do I come to get my fare paid home?"

Another quick look. His eyes narrowed. "Your fare paid home? Wait a minute . . . didn't he send you money for carfare down here? You should have had a check or a ticket to come down."

"Yessir. He sent me a check. It came last month. But we had to use it to put a new roof on the farm. That big storm last winter like to blow it off and I couldn't leave Grandma. So when it came time to report I just borrowed the money from her."

"Off your grandma? You live with your grandma?"

"Yessir. My father's dead, and my mother died two years ago. So I sort of wondered if I'd get sent back . . . or not. . . ."

"Well, you'll be paid something while you're down here."

"Yessir, I know, but that goes home to Grandma. Y'see I had a job at MacKenzie's drugstore, but when I quit 'course my pay there stopped."

"So you want to know if you'll be sent back to your job?"

"No, sir. Mr. MacKenzie, he said he wasn't holding jobs open for ballplayers. He gave the job to Jimmy Harrison. I just want so's I can take care of Grandma."

"I getcha. Well, I shouldn't worry if I were you. We'll see you land some place. Maybe if we can't use you there'll be a spot for you in one of our farms. Just you go in there and pitch the kind of ball you did the day I saw you last summer. And don't worry about getting home, understand?"

"Thanks, Mr. MacManus. Thanks lots. That sure helps. I'll be in there trying every minute." Now the sun really was shining. He felt warm and happy because the worst load of all was taken from his mind. Somehow, some way, they'd see he got back to Grandma. Who knows; maybe he might make good after all? Might be able to buy a blue sports coat with blue striped pants and white shoes. And a big car with the top rolled back to drive down all the way to the training camps in Florida. Who knows? There was almost a grin on the great man's face. He was smiling at someone.

"Hey, Jim, c'mon over here. Meet Roy Tucker, kid from Connecticut I was telling you about yesterday."

A small, thickset man coming out of the hotel yanked his hand from his side pocket. It was a flabby hand, not lean and hard like MacManus'. "Oh, yeah, you're the Boy Wonder from Connecticut, are you? Gladder see you. Well, you joined a screwy outfit all right." He looked the Kid up and down with a glance that was not unfriendly and not friendly either. Then he half turned his back, interested no more, and addressed MacManus.

"Say, Murphy just passed through. He stopped for breakfast. Drove down South, on some kind of scouting trip, for that Tiger second baseman, I guess. Know what he said?"

The face of the older man darkened at once. He became another person, full of unconcealed annoyance as he answered quickly:

"No, I don't. I don't care what he said. Don't bother to tell me. Let him mind his own business and I'll try to mind mine."

"Yeah, but you gotta hear this one. This is good, this is. He says the Dodgers'll win the pennant."

"This year?"

"Yep. This year."

"How's he figure that one?"

"Says there's gonna be war. That all the other teams will have to go and fight, but that most of the Dodgers will be too old . . ."

The annoyance that had changed into curiosity changed into anger. His face became red.

"Kindly tell Murphy to mind his own business and quit popping off about our chances, will you?" His voice rose. The Kid thought this a good chance to move out of the firing line, especially as the bus that was to take the squad to the ball park drew up just then with a creaking of brakes. He heard the last few words. . . .

"Tell him I'm running my ballclub, and if he doesn't mind . . ."

3

A gray-haired man in a dingy shirt and a blue baseball cap well down over his eyes shoved an armful of clothes at the Kid and indicated his locker. "Fifty-six. In the back row, there." The lockers were plain wooden stalls about six feet high with a shelf one or two feet from the top. The front of his locker was open and along the edge at the top was pasted:

"TUCKER. NO. 56."

There was his uniform with the word "DODGERS" in blue across the front and the number 56 on the back of the shirt. Already he had discovered there were twelve pitchers trying for half a dozen places, most of them with some experience, several like Kennedy and Foster and Rats Doyle with years in the League behind them. So what chance did a rookie have? But that blue cap and the shirt with the word "DODGERS" he could take home to prove that once he had trained with a big-league team.

The crowd dressed noisily, shouting and yelling across the little clubhouse. Finally when they were all dressed the door shut with a bang and a small, active little man with thinning yellow hair rasped out a few sentences. The Kid knew him immediately. It was Gus Spencer; "Gabby Gus" as everyone called him, the new manager, the best fielding shortstop in the League, once of the famous Gas House Gang, terror of opposing baserunners, the pet hate of all umpires and the kind of a fighting ballplayer who would rather scrap than eat. The squad grouped around and listened, some with grave and serious faces, others with a faint smile as if it were an old story. They sat on the benches before the lockers, they knelt on chairs or stood behind, peering over shoulders, while he talked in a voice that commanded the situation, that compelled them to listen whether they wanted to or not, as with his cap now off, now slung nervously on the back of his head, he gesticulated with his hands.

". . . and only one practice a day; only one practice, so put everything you got into it. Remember I wanna hustling ball team. They's some fellas can't do anything but play ball and they're too gosh-darned lazy to do that. We don't want 'em down here. Now get out and le's see some pepper, pepper, y'unnerstand. . . ."

Only one practice a day! One practice a day wasn't so bad, thought the Kid as the door flew open and they swarmed onto the field. Clack-clack, clackety-clack, clack-clack their spikes sounded on the concrete floor of the porch.

"One squad on the mats, the other at the wands." At first he didn't know what was meant until he saw they were divided into two groups and his was to take exercise first on a string of mats laid out in a line on the ground. Gosh, the sun was bright. It blinded him as he looked up. Then he lay on the mat and, at the command of a short man in white trousers and a white undershirt, began the exercises. "One-two, one-two, up . . . down . . . up . . . down . . . one-two, one-two . . ." The leader had an unpleasant way of yanking your legs sharply into position or pushing them back if you didn't do the exercise properly or weren't keeping in time, and he kept walking around watching everyone, seeing that each man got into each exercise. These were not ordinary exercises, either. They were movements that brought to life new muscles, that took hold of you in queer places, exercises the like of which the Kid had never done before. The squad lay on their backs, bending their torsos up and down, kicking the right leg sideways, the left leg sideways, turning almost completely over, coming back, fast, faster, as the little man shouted his commands. Above the hot sun of Florida began the process of conditioning. Sweat poured down their faces, grunts and gasps became louder and louder, yet that demon in the undershirt and white pants kept them going steadily. No letup.

"One-two, one-two, twist, turn, one-two, one-two . . ."

Half an hour of this torture and then they rose for another thirty minutes of drill with wands. The first exercises they had taken on their backs, but this one they did upright. Holding long wands by each end they slipped them over the back of their necks, and knelt, turned, twisted, and bent to the orders of another leader, a tall, dark-haired man who also knew his business. He too was pitiless, he also roared his commands without giving them a moment to breathe between exercises.

"Dip, bend, dip, bend, dip, left, right, get together there, you men in the last row . . . dip, bend, left, right . . ."

The sun beat upon them. The sun sank into their necks and faces. It was warmer at eleven-thirty than at ten-thirty, and so were they. One fat man collapsed completely and slunk into the clubhouse to the sound of jeers. Others coughed, wheezed, and puffed through the exercises, somehow, anyhow. The Kid wondered whether he could last. He wanted terribly to stop, felt like throwing it all up, like going home, but yet he held on. The torture never seemed to end, always that eternal "One-two, one-two, now up, down . . ." until at last the welcome words: "All right, you men. Coupla brisk laps and you'll be ready for practice."

Ready for practice! The Kid was ready to quit.

Following the two laps came a pepper game. Behind home plate and lined up against the backstop of the grandstand the squad spread out in two lines some thirty feet apart. Now the Kid had often taken part in pepper games, so-called, but this was different. This was the real thing and no mistake. One line was armed with bats. The other line threw the ball and the batters smacked it back at them with all their force. You had to be quick to avoid that deluge of balls coming at you from a distance of thirty feet.

They came smack at your face, over your head so you had to leap for them, at your toes, the ball taking a wicked bound as you got down to it, and as soon as you had thrown it, there it was back at you. Moreover, balls of the men on either side came your way and often you were catching one ball and dodging another. It was speed, speed, speed. No wonder a player was through in a few years.

In ten minutes the Kid ached all over. Never before had he realized the difference between big-league ball and the bush league variety. If you lived through six weeks of this sort of thing you were a ballplayer.

It was several days before he really got a chance to warm up. His catcher was a brown-eyed, older man with a nice face who smiled agreeably as they started tossing the ball back and forth. The Kid threw a few easily, but the exercises had stiffened him up, for there was a slight twinge in his arm above the elbow. Or was it merely the fact that those muscles had not been used since the previous fall? He pushed the ball and glove automatically under his left armpit and began rubbing his right arm vigorously.

Instantly the catcher walked quickly toward him. "Arm sore?"

"Not sore exactly, seems a little weak. . . ."

"All right. That's not such a bad sign the first few days. Throw some from here." He was standing about half the regulation distance of sixty feet, and the Kid tossed him the ball. This was easier. He threw another, and another at the short range. Before long the twinge was gone. His arm felt looser the more he pitched, and inside of ten minutes he was able to put a little steam into it. The catcher motioned him. "Now try it from here again." And he went back the regulation distance to the plate sunk into the ground. "But be sure and take it easy."

The longer distance didn't bother him at all, for his arm was warm now and the muscles limbered up. He felt easier the more he pitched, but he realized that the first few weeks he'd have to go slow. Pretty soon the catcher came up, the ball in his mitt. There were men pitching on both sides and the Kid presumed he had done something wrong and was going to be called. But the brown-eyed man smiled.

"Show me how you hold that ball."

The Kid showed him. "All right. That's fine if it's comfortable and you're used to it. But just try it this way a few times. You'll soon find you get lots more stuff this way." He held the ball with his two forefingers over the top seam. "Try this now, and see how it goes."

Yes, to his surprise he had more stuff. His control was better. The catcher grinned approvingly. "See how it helps? You can do things with a ball that way." He walked halfway to the box, then turned. "Hope you don't mind my telling you. My name's Leonard. I've been catching in this League almost twenty years."

The Kid felt embarrassed. His mouth was hot and dry and his voice broke as he answered. Mind? This certainly wasn't his idea of the big leagues, a veteran catcher being considerate with a young rookie, taking all that trouble with

HE WAS ABLE TO PUT A LITTLE STEAM IN IT

a pitcher who might last a few weeks in training camp. "Mind? No . . . I sh'ld say not. I'm much obliged. It's better, that grip." The catcher nodded and tossed him the ball. For twenty minutes more they continued until stopped by a fierce whistle from the dugout.

"That's enough out there . . . you pitchers . . . c'mon in and get some batting practice."

"Try that again tomorrow," said the catcher. "See, when you get that twist over the seam you're able to put more stuff on the ball, understand? Throw it at his knees."

The Kid thanked him and went for his bat. His own beloved bat. He found it and stood behind the screen waiting his turn at the plate. Pitching he liked, but batting he loved. He loved the sensation of outguessing another man in the box, of catching a fast one cleanly on the nose and cracking through a hole in the infield, loved even the hearty swing when he missed a curve. He took his place in the batter's box. The pitcher wound up, he swung . . . and missed. . . .

There was a low outside ball and then he got a good, full smack and sent it screaming into deep right center. The next he caught on the nose too, a deep fly, a deep ball to right . . . no . . . a couple of fielders were backing up . . . over the fence. Short, that fence, only 275 feet. But over nevertheless.

The pitcher rubbed up another ball. He was a tall, rangy, powerful fellow, a fresh rookie, anxious to show something. He looked at the plate a few seconds, nodded to the catcher, wound up . . . and . . . it came at the Kid's head. He swung back and away, tripped clumsily over his bat and fell sprawling on the ground. Someone behind the cage said something, and there was laughter. So they thought he was scared? Well, he was. He picked himself up, got his bat from the ground where it had rolled, then, flushed and hot, stood up again at the plate. The ball came high once more, and he caught it cleanly. Back it went, back . . . back . . . and over the center field fence, the furthest from the plate.

The little blond-haired man came up to him. He barked, but it was a friendly bark.

"Howsa arm? . . ."

"Okay."

"All right. You better get in now. Take a coupla laps."

The Kid jogged twice round the edge of the field and ended up in a walk near the clubhouse in left. It was well after one o'clock, but even with three hours of solid practice men were still stopping grounders in the infield, chasing flies near the fence, batting or catching the ball, all running at full tilt. Three hours of speed, speed, speed. He wondered how they could stand it, because he himself was almost all in. A few didn't. Here and there stragglers were coming in loudly demanding a Coke, others were undressing inside as he completed the circuit of the park and came onto the porch of the clubhouse. Standing there was a tall fellow with shoulders like a taxi, negligently leaning against a post and talking to a couple of men in civilian clothes. Someone just behind the Kid mumbled a name. Nugent. Of course, Nugent! He recognized him by the pictures in the papers. Razzle-Dazzle Nugent, the great Brooklyn pitcher who was a hold-out.

Carelessly exchanging jokes with his companions, the great man stood at his ease, a poem in gray. He wore a gray double-breasted sports suit belted in the back, a gray felt hat tilted over one eye, a gray silk sports shirt open at the neck, and gray suède shoes. The Kid's heart sank as he passed close behind him and, seeing the powerful shoulders, realized the strength of his muscles. Razzle-Dazzle who had won fifteen games with a last place club, and was holding out for a ten-thousand-dollar raise.

The Kid passed inside and started pulling off his steaming clothes. "Well, boy," said the gray-haired man, "I seen you take a coupla belts at that old apple. Whatcha tryin' for?"

"Pitcher," he grunted in reply, so tired it was an effort even to grunt.

"Pitcher!" The man looked at the sign on top of the locker. "Tucker? Oh, you're that Kid from Tomkinsville, ain't you? Yeah, well, you got a good easy swing at the plate for a pitcher, all right. Get into that-there shower now."

Under the hot relaxing shower full of sweating men, and then out to dress slowly. Clack-clack, clackety-clack, the rest of the gang came pouring in from the field. Now the room reeked with the smell of sweaty clothes and odor of ointments from the rubbing tables at the side. The old man was writing on the wall as he came out of the shower.

"EVERYONE REPORT IN UNIFORM AT 10:30 TOMORROW."

The Kid dressed slowly and came out on the porch to wait for the bus to take them back to the hotel. One practice a day. One practice a day didn't sound so much when you said it fast at ten-thirty in the morning, but now he couldn't have walked a hundred yards. It was the continual speed which cooked a guy. That afternoon he would take things easy, go out to the beach and stretch out in the sand.

Others did the same thing. Meanwhile a conference was going on in room 805. There was the great man himself with his feet on a table, there was the little man who gave the exercises, and the manager, all three reddened by the tropical sun of the morning.

"By the way, Gus, you happen to notice that rookie whale some of those balls this morning?"

The blond man barked back, "Yeah, I seen 'em, but that don't mean nothing. Not a thing. Pitchers ain't putting anything on the ball yet. You know how 'tis. First few days . . ."

"Sure I know. I know jes' as well as you do. But his swing, I mean. The way he leaned into that second homer. D'ja notice that?"

While some of the squad, after a late lunch, went to the beach and while that conference was going on in room 805, the veteran catcher who had shown the Kid how to hold the ball, took the elevator straight to his room on the fifth floor, locked himself in and, taking off his clothes, got into bed. He stretched out, tired and lame in every joint. Ah . . . that was good. Thirty-eight and almost twenty years in the League. Now he felt his age. Baseball was a game of speed. The slight confidence he had before practice had vanished, wiped out by those three hours of exercise in the burning sunshine. He was exhausted. Couldn't fool himself. Only one practice a day. But another practice at 10:30 tomorrow.

4

Working in MacKenzie's drugstore on the corner of South Main at home the weather was the weather, something to which he paid no particular attention. It was hot: it was cold: it rained: it snowed; but except on Saturdays and Sundays in midsummer when he was pitching for the team, the weather didn't count. At Clearwater he soon discovered that the weather was vitally important. For ballplayers the weather is everything. After the first few days he began to feel the rigorous exercise and the regime of work under the sun and longed for a day or two of rain. Unfortunately in Florida it never rained.

Always the sun. Always the sun beating upon them as they bent, dipped, and twisted on those mats in those agonizing exercises; one-two, one-two, up . . . down . . . up . . . down . . . get together there, you men in the third row. The only variation in the program came later in the practice when Gabby Gus started to emphasize defensive tactics. In turn each pitcher took the mound. He threw to the plate, and as he did so a coach rapped out a grounder between the box and first, well to the side of first. The pitcher then had to run across and cover the bag, taking the throw from the first baseman. All the time Gus stood on the coaching lines, criticizing, yelling at each man, hustling them every minute.

"C'mon there, Tucker, whassa matter, get that lead out of yer pants. Le's have some of the ol' pep now. Lil speed. Faster, much faster. Try it again. All right. . . . HEY . . . don't watch me. Whatcha watching me for? You're watching me. Watch Kennedy. Jake—show him how." The veteran threw the ball and galloped over to the bag, looking up at the exact moment to catch the first baseman's throw.

"See . . . try it once more. No, wait a minute. You gotta run hard and take the ball two strides before you get to the bag. Now once more . . . speed, speed . . . tha's more like it . . . try it again. . . ." And again. And again until the Kid was so whipped and winded and exhausted he could hardly stand.

Following that was half an hour's sliding practice for the whole team. The sliding pit was in deep right field behind the foul lines, and Gabby stood at the side explaining and pointing out each man's faults as he came into the bag. From a spot fifteen yards distant the runner started hard, and when he neared the pit Gabby would call "left" or "right" according to which side he wanted the man to slide. It was hot work, dirty and dusty work, and Gabby was merciless. First the hook slide in which the runner hooked the bag with one leg with the slide on the other thigh and leg.

"Now, boys, you're out at the plate, see. Come into it with both feet. And show some speed, will ya. . . ." Player after player came crashing in, trying to upset one of the coaches who stood over the bag. Sliding was easy for the Kid. He'd been taught and well taught by his high school coach and had no difficulty following orders and changing direction at the last second, but some of the men got so rattled and upset they couldn't slide properly.

"Now, then, you pitchers." Gabby had no mercy. No intention to let them rest a second despite the heat and the sun. "Line up here, you pitchers." And he sent them all off on a race into deep left field. This was the pastime the Kid enjoyed, for with his long legs he was able to beat the others. When they were strung out in the field one of the coaches started batting fungo flies. Charlie Draper could drop a fungo on a dime at three hundred feet, and he invariably managed to make each man run himself to the limit to catch the ball. When anyone tried to sneak a start on him, the hitter deftly poked the ball a little further.

The business of warming up his arm was not enjoyable for the Kid. To be sure, it was somewhat of a physical rest; but the mere sight of those other pitchers, all with curves and fast balls, all sure of themselves and their places, was anything but encouraging. Halfway through practice he looked up to see the friendly older man, the veteran catcher who had caught him the first morning, standing at his side. It was Leonard who spoke first.

"I've been watching you. You got a natural,

easy motion there. Take care of yourself and you'll last a long while."

The Kid threw a fast ball. It zoomed over the plate and into the catcher's glove. Those words and the friendly tone made him feel better. The older man continued.

"One thing you'll hafta learn though. You're in the big leagues and if these guys can spot your stuff they'll hit it a mile and a half. Or the coaches will steal it and tip off the batters. Wait a minute . . . just watch old Fred out there. See . . . he hasn't got much stuff, but he hides the ball so well the batter never knows what's coming. He throws from his hip pocket. Lots of effective pitchers haven't got so much stuff as some, but they know how to use it. Watch him there . . . see how his glove covers up the ball when it comes up . . . notice . . . see, like this. . . ."

He took the ball and showed how it should be concealed, how to hold your glove over it, while once again the Kid wondered that a veteran catcher would bother to take time to explain things of this kind to a rookie pitcher. These were the moments he felt the big league wasn't so bad after all. Then the squad was called in for batting practice, after which they were divided into three teams of eleven or twelve men each and ended with a relay race in which everyone including Gabby and the coaches took part. The Kid was exhausted as they finally walked to the clubhouse for a Coke and a shower. He said so to the man at his side.

"I'm all in. They sure work their pitchers hard on this man's team."

"Hey?" It was Charlie Draper, the coach. "Boy, you ain't seen nothing yet. Gabby has a theory, he has. He says now . . . if you develop a pitcher's legs you cut down the chances of injury to his arms about fifty per cent. He says the reason is clear enough if you stop to figure it out. If a pitcher has weak legs or something goes wrong with one of 'em, he naturally puts more strain on his arm to get his stuff across. Don't he? Sure he does; all right, strengthen his legs and what happens? The strain comes off his arm and becomes equally distributed in a smooth body action. See?"

Well, they were certainly doing it. Even Razzle, Razzle the great, who had held out for three days and then only signed up the night before, had to go through the same grind. The Kid noticed also that Gabby never spared himself. On the contrary, he covered twice as much ground as anyone on the squad. Now he was with the pitchers in left field, now at the sliding pit in right, now conversing with MacManus on the clubhouse porch, now behind the batting screen watching the newcomers take their swings. He took the same exercise. If there was batting practice, he was in getting his raps; he was all over the park, watching everyone, barking out orders, shouting to the pitchers to go easy there, taking his turn at the plate. Whenever a player made a bobble Gus saw it. "You ain't getting down in front of the ball, Tony," to an infielder who let a grounder roll through his legs. Gabby didn't miss a thing.

Among the mob of players, strange faces which seemed stranger still in uniform, one or two persons began to stand out. MacManus, Jake Kennedy, an old-timer who wore a gold band with a large diamond in it, a World Series ring won years before with the Giants, Leonard the catcher who had been so helpful, Draper the coach, Doc Masters the trainer, a small slightly deaf man who couldn't hear if you asked him whether Nugent was likely to sign up but could hear clean across the lobby of the Fort Harrison when someone asked him to have a cigar. These men were personalities and he began slowly to sort out a few other faces too.

But save for those few and his roommate, a boy from Dallas, the rest of them were unknown. He was confused and bewildered by their clothes, by their ease and informal manners, the way they could glance at a menu as long as your arm and order immediately what they wanted, strange dishes of which the Kid had never heard. Their talk was of strange names and strange places too; cities they had played in and lived in, cities they liked or disliked. Beside his solemn-faced roommate he sat silently alone at a table for four. Day after day he took this empty table while the others passed by and walked over to tables of their friends where he could hear them talking.

"Heat . . . say, boy, you-all should have seen Beaumont. We sure like to die down there . . . all the other teams in the League played night ball, but we had to play by day . . . yessir, but lemme tell you one thing, in St. Louis once it was a hundred-eighteen in the dugout. . . . Boy, it's sure hot in that town. . . . I'm telling you. . . . How 'bout Louisville? Or Atlanta? Them's the two worst towns in the country, I reckon. . . . Indianapolis . . . you ain't known heat till you played there. . . . Heat, why, you guys dunno what you're talking 'bout. Down my way in Oklahoma it's hot. . . . Ah mean hot. It's so hot when a dawg chases a rabbit they both walk. . . ."

Louisville. Beaumont . . . Indianapolis. Minor league towns. Tank towns in the minors. He glanced at the serious face of the boy across the table and the boy glanced back, for they were thinking the same thought. Those were the places they'd be sent to play in, if indeed they made good at all. One hundred and eighteen in the dugout . . . no, that was St. Louis. So hot a dawg chases a rabbit. . . . Beaumont . . . Atlanta . . . Kansas City . . . Those towns seemed far away; they accentuated his loneliness more than ever. He pushed back his chair and reached in his pocket for a quarter to leave for the waitress. A quarter was a lot of money if you stopped to think it over. Why, in MacKenzie's drugstore on the corner of South Main, you got a meal for a quarter. But that was what all the players left: twenty-five cents. He walked out to the elevator, something in the distant sky recalling a sunset at home, and he remembered he hadn't written to Grandma for two days. She wrote him every single day. The sunset brought up a vision of the sky over the fresh green lower meadow in spring. He decided he didn't exactly feel like writing. But anything was better than the stuffy empty bedroom over the noisy street. So he went down into the lobby, got paper and an envelope, and began with a hotel pen.

"Dear Grandma . . ."

5

By the end of the first week practice was livened by inter-squad games. This didn't mean practice was shortened; not at all. The two teams went five or six innings after the regular workout, and those half dozen men who didn't get in were supposed to watch carefully. Consequently the squad seldom returned to the hotel before two-thirty or three in the afternoon.

Hopefully the Kid sat on the bench every day. The pitchers were only permitted to go a couple of innings and each morning he waited patiently for the call which didn't come. Harry Street, his roommate, got in at shortstop for several innings, however, and made two clean hits in his two times at bat off Jake Kennedy, the veteran pitcher. He was a queer, silent youth, quietly confident of his own ability, his value to baseball and the team, and his ultimate success. A wonderful pair of hands added to his natural speed. The Kid would have given lots for that kind of temperament. Harry never had any fears or worries and none of the loneliness which beset him in the midst of that noisy crowd. When their lights were out at night and they lay abed discussing the day's play, his roommate always ended on the same note.

"Aw . . . I can hit any righthander in this-here league." Then he would turn over and be asleep in five minutes. The next morning the Kid would watch him stalk confidently up to the plate and show himself as good as his word.

While the Kid was sitting on the bench, consumed by doubts. Mowing down the Cuban Giants was one thing; but how would he go against these hitters? Nor did the opportunity to test himself come, either. Another day, and another, and another went past. The inaction was awful, and gradually he felt his small store of confidence oozing away as pitcher after pitcher was thrown into the short practice games each morning and he still sat watching. To be sure, he took his turn throwing to the hitters in practice, but as the squad lined up in the field he was on the bench again. The only part of practice which he enjoyed was the race. At the end of the workout the squad was lined up for a race across the field, and he was always first or second to Harry Street, the fastest man on the club. Beating Harry gave him a kick, and he looked forward to the race every morning.

But he didn't look forward to practice. Continued inaction was sapping his morale and he dreaded the time he might have to step out there, hoping they'd release him or send him away before he made a fool of himself in the box. This was his attitude when he saw Gabby Spencer, the manager, coming across the hotel lobby to where he was sitting mournfully one night.

"Howsat ol' arm, Tucker, okay? Yeah? Mebbe I'm gonna shove you in there a few innings tomorrer."

The Kid went upstairs. He could hardly sleep all night. At last, a chance against the big-league hitters! What he'd been hoping for since he landed in Clearwater, and now that the moment had come he was frightened. He always remembered that next morning, because after he reached the field and got dressed he came out of the clubhouse to a strange sight. Half a dozen photographers were snapping Razzle Nugent, the star pitcher who had been a hold-out all spring. Instantly the Kid realized something. Those wonderful pictures one saw on the sports pages were mostly posed. They were fakes! Those shots of fielders making one-handed catches, of first basemen stretched out on the bag, of runners sliding headlong into base, were phony. Razzle lay on a mat upon his back. Above him leaned the trainer rubbing an enormous medicine ball across his stomach. Around one side and from every position stood the cameramen, two of them mounted on a packing box, others standing on chairs or kneeling beside the mat. Then that piercing whistle called them to practice. As he walked across the diamond he heard someone say,

"Yeah, they're getting Razzle 'cause he's going in a few innings for the first time this morning." Nugent was pitching against him. A chance to beat the great Razzle, to bring himself to the attention of the owner sitting there on the clubhouse porch, the newspapermen scattered over the press box, and Gabby himself. If it had only happened ten days before! Now he was worried and uncertain.

There was the usual warm-up, the pepper practice, and after that he took a few swings at the plate. Then the whistle blew. The two teams started the game and once more the Kid found himself in the bullpen, eagerly watching each move, waiting for the call. It came in the third inning when Gabby pulled out Rats Doyle, who was puffing and blowing in the hot sun, and shouted out from the coaching lines,

"Hey there . . . Tucker." The Kid jumped. Thump-thump went his heart. Here was his chance at last. He knew Razzle would be sent in for the regulars and already he could see the headlines in the next morning's sports pages. "Razzle Nugent Beats Rookie Pitcher." However, he was starting with a three to one lead in his favor, so he walked out to the box, hoping that he wouldn't disgrace himself in his first try.

Unfortunately pitching to these men was different. They had an annoying habit of standing there motionless, their bats on their shoulders, refusing to bite at anything wide, just waiting, waiting . . . and then when a good one came, smacking it. Fast fielding saved him in the first inning he pitched. But when he finally came out after three innings, the score was eight to three for the regulars. His roommate put the finishing touch by cracking him for a double to score two men, and then, dancing off second, stole third under the Kid's eyes. It was his fault, entirely his fault and not the catcher's. He longed for the

IT WAS OVER THE FENCE

confidence of that brown-eyed boy jumping off third.

"Watch yourself there . . . watch yourself," shouted the coach back of third as the youngster hopped up and down the basepath, arms outstretched.

"Yeah," retorted the brash rookie. "Well, I got here on my own and I'll get home on my own too." A titter went round the diamond at the expense of Charlie Draper, the third base coach. In the box the Kid heard the retort and winced. That was the kind of temperament to have. Meanwhile Allen, the big burly first baseman, apparently afraid of nothing, known for his ability to hit any sort of ball, stood menacingly at the plate. In desperation the Kid put everything he had into his pitch. He wound up, the batter met the ball, the fielders backed up . . . it was over the fence. He heard the call from the first base coaching line.

"Norman, le's see what you can do out there." The Kid came back slowly, stuffed his glove into his hip pocket, put on his jacket, and walked round back of the plate to the clubhouse. He knew what they were saying in the dugout as he went past. Seven runs, three bases on balls, and Heaven knows how many hits. In three innings. A knot of men on the clubhouse porch were watching the game and talking. They paid no attention as he passed and he heard someone say,

'Jes' the same, if Gabby wasn't a fixture at short I'd say it would be hard to keep that fresh busher off the team." They were talking about

Harry, his roommate. As he went inside to the showers, typewriters were clattering merrily in the press box beside the clubhouse. The press, anxious to be off fishing, and unanimously bored, were writing the leads to their daily stories without waiting for the end of the game. In fact some of them had completed their chore, and Casey was shoving in his last sheet.

"The biggest disappointment of the day's play was that peerless leader, Manager Gabby Gus Spencer, at shortstop. If his play today was a sample, MacManus ought to ship him to Tulsa in the Texas League. Had Gabby only been a little better, he'd have been lousy. An eighteen-year-old busher named Harry Street on the rookies showed the old man up both in the field and at the bat.

"I've always had a suspicion that Gabby talks a better game of ball than he plays. Now I know it. Wonder where he wants that wheel-chair sent? You can have my share of Gabby if you give me young Street, and I'll throw in Tony Galento and One-eyed Connolly too. With this bunch of sapadillos, Gabby will be lucky not to end up by the Fourth of July in the International League. He had three pitchers in there this morning throwing the ball all over the park except at the plate, and young Tucker, the sensational Kid who was to pitch the team into the World Series, tried his luck for the first time and delivered up seven runs in three innings.

"However, there's one thing about our Dodgers. I'd rather watch them run past each other on the base line and go to sleep on the sacks than watch the Yanks win a doubleheader without a run scored against them. When the Yanks play you know what'll happen. With the Dodgers anything can happen. And usually does."

6

When the Kid reached the hotel tired and discouraged, there was a big pile of mail waiting for him. Seemed as if everyone in Tomkinsville was writing. Everyone at home, they said, was interested in him, even old Mr. Haskins, the president of the First National Bank, who had told him he'd be unwise to leave his job at MacKenzie's because he shouldn't associate with ballplayers; yes, even Mr. Haskins was reading the sports pages in hopes of seeing his name. . . . Everyone was following his progress. Did he think Brooklyn would win the pennant? What about Razzle Nugent, the hold-out? Would he sign up? When was the Kid going to start a game and show those birds up? There were a dozen foolish questions in every letter. He wished they hadn't written at that particular minute. One after the other, he opened and read them; each one hurt. Up to a lunch which he couldn't eat, and then to the beach alone. He returned early to dinner so he wouldn't have to face the other players. It was after eight and he was sitting alone in the dark room when a knock sounded at the door. He leaned over quickly and put on the light.

"C'mon in. . . ."

The door opened and Leonard, a toothpick in his mouth, entered. He saw a solemn-faced boy hunched up in a chair by the window overlooking the front porch and the cars swarming past on the main street of Clearwater below.

"Hullo there. Thought I'd drop in a minute." He closed the door carefully and came inside.

"Uhuh. Sit down, won't yuh?" Ordinarily he would have been delighted to have seen the old catcher, but not that night. That night he wanted to be entirely alone.

"Well, things didn't go so good out there for you this morning, did they?"

The Kid didn't want to talk about it, or even to think about it, but all of a sudden he discovered that he did want to talk. "No, sir. They sure didn't. I don't know what it was; I didn't have any control."

The older man nodded and the toothpick did a little dance. "I know. That's often how it is. Well, it's not the first time you been belted I guess, nor the last time either. Pitching against real hitters is tough, especially at first. You'll get used to them. I think I might have helped you if I'd been in there, once or twice . . . that time you grooved that ball for Allen."

He nodded his head. That was a bad mistake. "Yeah, thought I'd fool him."

"These boys are smart. But that's how it is." There was a pause, an awkward silence as the toothpick flipped across his mouth. Suddenly the old catcher leaned forward. "You feel right sorry

"YOU FEEL RIGHT SORRY FOR YOURSELF, DON'T YOU?"

for yourself sitting here all alone in the dark, don't you, son?" Now how on earth did he know that? How did he know the lights were off? No, the Kid certainly wasn't happy, flopping in his first chance in the big leagues, his only chance, maybe. The visitor leaned back in his chair and the toothpick did another fascinating little dance across his mouth. "Well, I'm gonna tell you something. An' I mean it. You got the making of a good player. You can hit, and I think you can pitch. Only one thing. It's up to you."

"Up to me?"

"Yep. . . . Like this, now. A fella gets out of baseball just what he puts into it, unnerstand? Any boy with arms, legs, and a good heart can break into the big leagues. I think . . . ah . . . now I think you've got them. Maybe I'm wrong."

Arms. Legs. A good heart.

"But I don't believe I am wrong. I'm not wrong on rookies very often. Lemme tell you something. Unless a kid has awful tough breaks, like he has a sprained ankle or a bum leg, or there's some star in the position he's after, see . . . this boy Street is trying for the manager's job at short . . . well, unless there's something like that, any youngster who's fast and can throw and can stand up to the plate should make the grade. If he has one thing. Y'know, I've seen lots of ballplayers, lots that had everything except courage. They just didn't have it. And they wouldn't work. Pink Benton, for instance, when I was with the Senators, remember him? One of the best rookies ever I hope to see. Young. Strong as an ox. A good hitter, but no dash, no speed. Lead in his tail. Everyone had the tag on him. Just another ballplayer." There was a significant pause again. Then he said dryly, "He's with Fort Worth now."

The Kid began to understand. Before he could answer, the catcher went on. "Take Gabby, right here on this club. Gabby . . ."

This was too much. The Kid had been watching Gabby closely for two weeks, and, despite his poor play that morning, he had respect for the manager's ability. "Say, that guy's one swell ballplayer; he's a Fancy Dan out there in the field."

"Sure he is. Why? How'd he get to be manager. Never hit .300 in his life. Not too hot in the field. But he's been in the big leagues over ten years now and going stronger than ever. The answer's easy. Gabby has what it takes. Something, well, maybe something inside, if you get me. He isn't a great ballplayer, but he's full of pepper all the time, and salt too, and vinegar, yes, sir, plenty of it. Fancy Dan? Say, Fancy Dans are a dime a dozen out there round short. Gabby has something else. Fight, get me? He's scrapped more than the rest of this squad put together. Why, that guy has gone further with less in baseball than any player in either league."

Gradually the Kid began to understand. To understand baseball, what it really was, what it took. Here he was sitting in the dark, feeling sorry for himself and thinking about Grandma and the farm, when all the time he ought to be forgetting what had happened and getting ready for another day. Now he began to have an appreciation of the game, of what it was all about, of how players made themselves stars despite physical handicaps, some weakness in the field or at bat, despite drawbacks of various sorts. The toothpick continued its eternal dance as the older man leaned toward him.

"Look at Maranville. The Rabbit . . . never heard of him, hey? You have? Well, there was a little fellow about as big as a peanut, couldn't hit with a tennis racket, yet he was twenty years in the leagues. And old John McGraw . . . What made him a great player? Same thing, fight. And Frank Chance. Why, he used to do everything but walk out there and punch his own team on the nose to pep 'em up. Take Joe McCarthy. Never good enough to be a big leaguer himself. Just a scrub he was, once, yet when he finished everyone wanted to be on his team. And where are the great names of Joe's time, where are they now, hey?"

The kid had followed baseball all his life, loved the game, played it, yet for the first time he realized that more important than fielding or hitting, more important than anything, was that funny inner quality called courage. "Now take those pitchers out there chasing flies." The catcher tipped back his chair. "Take those catchers. I can always tell which ones are real ballplayers just by the way they run. That's why I got confidence in you. I watched you. You go all out every time, whether you nab that old apple or not. I watched you running that race every day; you get there first or pretty darn near it. That's the only reason I'm wasting my time here tonight. . . .

"Know what happened to you this morning?

Well . . . I'll tell you. You was choking up. The essence of pitching is one thing: co-ordination. You didn't have any. Naturally you didn't have stuff either. You were pressing, going too far back. I watched you carefully; you was throwing with your shoulder so far back it got in the way of your view. See? Listen, boy, I been through all this the same as you. Sure I've been through it; I remember when I broke in there was never anyone to tell me these things, though. No one ever told me my faults. I sat alone in a hotel room in the dark one night and saw myself with Utica on my shirt, the same as you. I had plenty of stumbles and tumbles. Only I kep' on a-plugging. I didn't quit, see; I didn't stop fighting. Look here, has a kid got it; that's all I wanna know. No scout can crack open a kid's head and find out, has he got guts. If he could, baseball would be a cinch. Every team would be the Yanks. So buck up, son. Forget this afternoon. Tomorrow's another day; get out there and play ball."

He walked toward the door, that toothpick still doing its everlasting turning and twisting in his mouth. Hand on the doorknob, he turned round.

"Son, an old umpire once give me some dope when I was a kid breaking in like you. Oh, yeah, I thought I was hot stuff, but they soon showed me I didn't have an idea what it was all about. Just when I got convinced I was a flop and waiting for that pink slip in the mail box, this old fella took me aside in the lobby of the hotel one night. Old George Connors, I never forgot. So I pass it along to you and don't you forget it either. 'Courage,' says this old-timer, 'courage is all life. Courage is all baseball. And baseball is all life; that's why it gets under your skin.'

"Good night!" The door slammed.

"Good night." The Kid jumped up from his chair. Tomorrow he'd show them. Tomorrow. He walked up and down the little room, the words of the older man in his ears. Of course, it was easier for old Leonard because he was a star, he was a fixture on the team, he wasn't just a cub trying to break into big-league ball. But still . . . to get discouraged, to get disheartened over one bad inning, that was foolish . . . that was . . .

How had the old catcher put it? Baseball is all courage . . . courage is all life . . . yep, that's right. Tomorrow. Tomorrow's another day.

7

It was the last game of the pre-season workouts and the team was playing the Indians. After that, one more day of practice and then the whole squad was to break camp at Clearwater and start the long, slow journey north, playing the Yanks every day in a different city and arriving in Brooklyn three days before the season began. As usual during games MacManus, his sunglasses shielding his eyes, his Panama carelessly placed on the back of his head, sat on a small wooden chair near the clubhouse porch back of the left field foul line. There was an empty chair on each side of him and from time to time some old player or one of the sportswriters from the press box behind third drifted over and sat down for a few minutes.

He was in a happy mood. The Dodgers had won two straight games from the Indians and this one was going well. At the end of the fourth the score was nothing to nothing and the Indians had not made a hit. It was Razzle Nugent's first game, and he was showing all his old stuff.

As the teams changed sides, the umpire turned to the stands.

"Pitching for Brooklyn . . . Roy Tucker, No. 56, in place of Nugent, No. 37. At short, Harry Street, No. 24, in place of Spencer, No. 4."

A tall man with glasses slipped into one of the empty seats. "Hullo there, Jack." It was Red MacDonald, manager of the Cincinnati team who had an off day. "Thought I'd drop over and see how you boys were doing? Who's that going in at short?"

"Hullo, Red. How are you? That? That's young Street. I picked him up in Muskegon last summer. Went up there to look over Mason, the outfielder with the Cubs, and saw this boy. Mind you, he's playing his first game in the big time, so he probably won't do much. Just watch him run though, that kid can run, lemme tell you. Say, when I watched him running for hits right in back of second I forgot all about Mason; yessir, I offered his manager two thousand for him right on the spot. Speed counts in this game."

"And that tall kid pitching now?"

"Tucker. He's another rookie. I got him in Waterbury, Connecticut, the same way. He was pitching one day against the Cuban Giants when I went up there to look at Simpson, their shortstop. This kid held 'em to one hit, and I signed him then and there and rushed him up to Elmira for the rest of the season. He doesn't know what it's all about yet."

MacDonald spat into the ground. "Well, there he starts to blow. . . ."

The first batter for the Indians received a base on balls. The Kid stood in the box with his legs apart as the first batter trotted down to first, and old Dave, his catcher, came out to him. Their heads went together a minute and the arm of the older man rested on his shoulder.

"Kinda wild, isn't he?" said MacDonald to the man next to him.

"We really don't know. This is the first game he's pitched and we wanted to see what he could do before we shipped him off to the farm. Fact is, he wanted to get in too. Last night he came round to Spencer's room and begged for a chance to pitch a few innings. I expect he's nervous out there for the first time. There she goes . . . there's a hit . . . oh . . . what a stop. . . ."

Davis, the Cleveland fielder, hit a beautiful line drive sharply over second, and the man on first was halfway down to the base when the shortstop ran over, leaped through the air, and with a backhanded stab caught the ball two inches from the dirt. He tumbled to the ground, rolled over, picked himself up with the ball in his hand, and threw to first for a doubleplay. The ball park roared. Catching the Indians in a doubleplay pleased the crowd.

A minute later the side was out and Street came in, tipping his cap. The Kid squeezed his arm as they slipped into the dugout. "Boy, you sure saved my bacon that time."

"Yeah . . . now le's go get some runs," said the confident youth, waving his bat. And old Leonard, taking off his pads, looked up at the Kid. "All right, boy, you put the ball where I told you. What? Sure you had luck; maybe you'll have some more. Keep cool and throw it where I say, that's all."

THREW TO FIRST

FOR A DOUBLEPLAY

In left field MacManus leaned back in his chair, lit a cigarette, his arms outstretched. He was pleased with himself and the world in general. "Yessir, that kid runs like a leaping gazelle, I'm telling you. Hullo there, Jim . . . how you like him?" This to Casey, the sportswriter, who came over and took the empty chair. "How's that for a stop, hey?"

"Looks as if maybe he might have something. I talked to him last night; say, he's full of pepper. Know what he says? Says, 'I can hit any right-handed pitcher in this here league.' 'Oh, yeah?' sez I; 'well, maybe you'll have a chance against Ruffing.' 'Okay,' he sez; 'I'll hit him.' How's that?"

"Well, he will, too. And he can bat from either side, remember."

"Can he? He ought to be a ballplayer one of these days. Who's that kid in the box now, Jack?"

"Roy Tucker. Lad from Tomkinsville; I was telling you about him."

"Oh, yeah, I remember. Has he been out all along? I haven't noticed he has much. And if that hotfoot out there in short hadn't picked up that liner he would have been scored on in the last inning. Now the rookie I like is young Jack Maguire with the Giants. . . ."

MacManus hurled his cigarette away. His face lost its contented look and he scowled as he turned on the sportswriter. "The Giants, the Giants, the Giants. You sportswriters give me a pain in the neck. Shoot, if a man wears a Giant uniform you all think he's hot stuff, and if he's on the Dodgers it doesn't matter how good he is.

Look at Caballero, this Cuban first baseman Murphy's trying out. I bet you five bucks he'll be out of the lineup by June, but the way they're playing him in the papers you'd think he was Greenberg and Gehrig and Hal Chase rolled into one. The Giants . . ." and he snorted as he crossed his legs and turned his back to the other man who winked at MacDonald and moved back to work in the press box while the teams changed sides.

"Okay, wait and see what Caballero does, that's all."

"I'll wait. The Giants!" said MacManus to the man next to him. "Those fellas are all alike. How you making out this year, Red?"

MacDonald thought he had a better team. So did every manager. "Say, Jack, how about Nugent? Think he can come back or not? I only watched the last inning."

MacManus became serious again. "Well, to tell the truth, Red, we don't know. This is the first time he's been in; you know he was a holdout the first ten days or so. Just now he's tending to business, and he pitched good ball today; his old fast one was burning in there. He's promised to cut out that wild stuff and play all season, and I think he will."

"When he's good that baby is sure good. But he gets mighty crazy when he starts to tear things up. How about this new man from Memphis, De Voe? And old Foster?"

"Can't tell yet about De Voe. Foster has just as much stuff as ever. What's the matter, looking for a pitcher?"

"I could use an extra one. How about this kid

in the box there? What you gonna do with him?"

"Send him along to Nashville, I suppose. Interested?"

"Not especially. I might be willing to take him off your hands though if the price was right."

"Like his motion? He's got an easy swing there, hasn't he?"

"Yeah," replied the other man without enthusiasm. "He's got a good swing. I like it."

"So do I," retorted the other with emphasis. Someone had been tipping Red off about the Kid, and if MacDonald wanted him enough to come up and watch him play, the boy was worth hanging on to. He turned back to the game. "Hullo, that's two strike-outs this inning. Red, you're pretty dumb. This kid will do all right when he gets some seasoning."

As inning after inning went on and neither team scored or made a hit, MacManus was unable to stand the strain. He rose nervously, walked over to the clubhouse porch, leaning against one of the posts of the roof. Then he lit a cigarette, threw it away half smoked, went back to his chair where he was now alone. He shoved his hat back over his head and a few minutes later pulled it down over his eyes. Harry Chase of the *Times*, watching from the press box, saw him twisting and turning in his chair. "Look at Jack over there; he's going nuts." And he rose and walked out into left field.

"Say, Jack, this boy looks pretty good to me. Why hasn't he been pitched before?"

"He was. They tried him out in a practice game once anyhow, and he didn't seem to have much. Fact we were about to give him his release last week, but Dave Leonard persuaded us to hang on to him, and then last night the kid talked Gabby into letting him go out there for a few innings this afternoon. They really wanted to see what Nugent would do, so he decided to let him try a couple of innings. I guess Leonard is making him out there."

"Maybe. He isn't making those fast balls though. Have you seen his stuff from behind the plate? You should see him from back there. Got control, too. Where'd you get him?"

He pulled his hat down over his eyes and flipped another half-smoked cigarette into the grass. "Up in Waterbury, a tank-town in Connecticut. I went to see Simpson, their shortstop, and this boy was pitching an exhibition game against the Cuban Giants. Seems he was some local boy from near there who was getting a try-out. He held 'em to one hit, and I said to Spike Davis, the manager, I said, 'Look here; I'll give you just exactly two thousand smackers for that son of a gun right here and now.' And he says, 'Well, two thousand's a lotta dough, but that boy has an awful big possibility,' and I said, 'Yeah, and so has two thousand in the bank. . . .' There she goes . . . there goes your ball game, Harry. . . ."

The batter hit a terrific drive into center. Scudder, the left fielder, was nearest the ball and went after it, running back and back. He came up against the fence as the ball descended. From the stands it looked over, but the fielder turned, leaped up, and literally pulled it down from the upper boards. It was a courageous catch and the whole crowd in the stands rose to him.

"Yessir, he's getting support all right." He lit another cigarette. "Some catch, boy," as Scudder trotted past. "Well, here we go, last of the ninth, no . . . that's only two out, isn't it? Who's up? Rogers? Say, what do you think of that? He has a chance of shutting these bums out without a hit." Once more he found it impossible to stand the strain, and pulling down his hat over his face, walked over to the clubhouse porch.

The batter with one strike and a ball stood waiting at the plate. He was looking for a fast one, but it was a curve and he swung well over the ball. His bat slipped from his hand, the ball rolling in the dirt toward third. Like a flash he was off while both the pitcher and the third baseman ran in for it; the pitcher, getting to it, stumbled momentarily, picked it up and threw it to first, a fraction of a second late to catch the runner. Hit number one for the Indians.

"Shoot," said MacManus. "I hoped the Kid would hold 'em down. Do those big bums good. And a scratch hit like that, too. Hang it, that would have done the boy a lot of good; given him all kinds of confidence." The catcher went down the line to the box and tossed the ball. There was silence on the diamond. Was this another ninth inning Indian rally? From the infield came the chatter of the team. "All right now, Roy, old kid, right in the slot. . . . Pretty lucky, that was, Roy. Give him both barrels, Roy. . . ." Then the voice of the umpire.

"Strike ONE. . . ."

"Thassa way to throw that old tomato, Tuck old boy. . . . That's pitching, that is. . . ." And a minute later the man on first started for second. Leonard's throw was perfect and the side was out, the Dodgers coming up for the last half of the ninth. Leaning against a post on the clubhouse porch, MacManus, with his left hand in his pocket and a cigarette in his other hand, walked nervously from side to side, coming back to his post as Casey ran across from the press box.

"Now what? Whad'I tell you, Jim? That kid has the makings." MacManus was pleased but he was especially pleased when he could prove a sportswriter, and above all, Casey, wrong. Easy enough to stand off and criticize. When you had the responsibility for the club, a responsibility to the stockholders too, well, it was different.

But Casey had heard it before. He was in a serious mood. With one hand he flipped open the scorebook he carried and shoved it at the other man. "Listen, Mac, you lucky bum, you know how many balls this kid has pitched in five innings? Twenty-six, that's all."

"Twenty-six called balls?"

"Twenty-six, only twenty-six, I counted 'em." He turned and went back to the press box, while MacManus shouted, "Where's MacDonald? Hey, Red, twenty-six balls he's pitched, only twenty-six. . . ."

Leonard was the first man up. He stood swinging his bat at the plate, while MacDonald, watching from left field, reminisced.

"Old Dave. Still a pretty good catcher, that old fella. I remember him back in the Series against the Tigers in '34. . . ."

"Yeah," the other interrupted. "That was in '34. A long while ago. He's old now, too old.

We want youngsters, and speed, see. Speed, that's gonna be the keynote of this team. A hustling ballclub. Like that kid coming to bat now."

Leonard had flied out, and Harry Street came to the plate. With a base on balls and two hits behind him, he caught the first ball pitched for a clean single to right center. MacManus poked his neighbor in the side.

"How's 'at, Red, three for three, and his first

big-league game. Say, if that kid was only with the Giants, can you imagine what they'd say?" He tossed his cigarette onto the grass with a gesture indicating his opinion of sportswriters, as he sat down again on one of the empty chairs. MacDonald came over and took another chair. Arms folded, silent but keen, the other man sat watching while MacManus twitched and crossed his legs. "Jack, I don't care, I'd just as leave make an offer for that boy if you'd care to listen."

"Which boy? Street? The lad on first?"

"Nope, that pitcher."

"Nosir. Nosir." He leaned over, tapped MacDonald on the arm and chest. "That kid has got something. Lemme tell you, Mac, the other night after we played the Tigers I found I'd left my reading glasses in the clubhouse. I was almost at the hotel, but I turned the car round and came back to get 'em. Doggone if it wasn't after six. The place was deserted except for this kid and old Fat Stuff Foster, you know, the old-timer. Fat was in there dishing 'em up to this boy, place almost getting dark, mind you. So I went up to him and says, 'Hey, you, what's the idea?' I says to this boy at the plate, 'I thought you were supposed to be a pitcher. What's the idea?' Know what he answers? 'Yessir, but I like to hit 'em too, and I'm weak on low balls. Besides I'm learning a new grip.' Whaddya think of that, hey? A pitcher and he likes to hit the ball!"

The batter hit a fast grounder to shortstop and the boy at first was well on his way to second. It was plain only an exceptionally fast throw would catch him, and MacManus half rose in his chair. "They'll have to be fast, they'll have to be fast . . ." he shouted exuberantly. "They'll have to be fast to catch that kid. . . . There . . . I told you . . . I told you . . ." as Street slid safely into second. "Whad'I say? He's a leaping kangaroo, that's what he is. Man on second, one out, winning run at the plate. Now, Kid, let's see what you can do; let's see you win your own game."

From deep left field they watched the tall, gangling boy shuffle up to the plate. He knocked the dirt from his spikes nervously, gripped his bat well up the handle, and stood legs apart on the edge of the box. "Makes you think kinda of Ted Williams, doesn't he?" said someone on the porch. From the dugout came the rattle and chatter of the Dodgers, and on the coaching lines calls and shouts reached the ears of the boy at the plate. "Attaboy, Tuck, take a cut at it . . . you can hit it. Roy old kid, old boy . . . make him come in there. Make him come in. Thassa boy . . . knock his turkey neck offen him, Roy . . ." He heard their voices and faced the ball. At last he was getting somewhere. He was one of them, one of the gang, not an outsider any more, but part of the machine, someone for whom they'd leap into the air and risk their necks by barging at full speed into the outfield fences. He was one of them and their actions said so; so too did the tone of their voices from the dugout behind him. The late afternoon sun beat on his burning neck as he watched the pitcher wind up and saw his leg rise. The ball was outside . . . and low . . . he leaned against it and felt the beautiful sensation of wood against ball.

The crowd rose with a yell. It was a hit, a long hit. Already Street was rounding third, his head down into his neck, while out in left field MacManus was dancing up and down. "Hey, Casey, how about it? No, sir, I'm not selling that kid, not a chance." Street neared home, he was crossing the plate, while the Kid got to second . . . but no further. He was surrounded. There were small boys who suddenly appeared from nowhere, there were fans pouring out of the low bleachers in right. There were the Indians running in to their dugout who paused to shake his hand. Half a dozen hands reached for his, from every side they were patting him on the back. In the press box back of third base the rat-tat-tat of the typewriters and the tap-tap of the telegraph bugs began furiously. In disgust Casey tore up a lead he had written before the game and put a fresh piece of paper into his machine. "Now whaddya think of that, Tom? Shut out by a rookie . . . one hit, too."

"By Jim Casey

"Today's news. The Dodgers have uncovered a pitcher at last. A nineteen-year-old rookie, Roy Tucker from Tomkinsville, Connecticut, pitching his first big-league game, went for six innings against the Indians here at Clearwater Park this afternoon, allowing one base on balls and one hit, of the scratch variety, struck out seven men, and pitched only twenty-six called balls. No, you don't have to believe it, this is a free country, but four thousand fans watched the Kid hold the Indians helpless as he tossed his fast ball at the command of veteran catcher Dave Leonard...."

Half an hour later the squad, or most of them, climbed into the bus to take them back to the hotel. The Kid was tired but wonderfully happy as he sat back and waited for the last inevitable slow dressers to clamber aboard. There was laughter and shouting and horseplay up and down the bus, everyone calling to him, yelling back at him and using his first name. The day before he was another one of those rookies; now he was Roy, and that's pitching, Roy, and, boy, you sure turned that old heat on them babies, Roy. Overnight he was theirs, he had arrived, he had become part of that secret fraternity, a baseball club. The bus started off slowly. Doc Masters, the trainer, asleep in a seat with the afternoon sun pouring in, snored gently. Someone reached over carefully and extracted the cigar case from the breast pocket of his coat. Half a dozen players helped themselves and then it was replaced with care.

"Hey, Doc, have a cigar. Have a cigar, Doc?" He woke as the bus swerved round the corner and into the main street of town. Sleepily he reached into his pocket to find his case empty, while they laughed and shouted at him, a happy bunch of boys. He grinned and shook his head. Kidding was all part of the game.

From his seat in the rear the rookie who had arrived listened to the talk and laughter. "Condition . . . Why, you couldn't get in condition if you was to run from here to Los Angeles. . . . Hey, Fat Stuff, wanna shoot some pool tonight? . . . Oh, Dave, what about those two bucks you bet me you'd get a hit today? . . . They wasn't nobody hitting; nobody except the pitchers. . . . I says to him, spring training is the toughest part of it. . . ."

Spring training the toughest part of it! He really believed it then, but later in the summer he would often wonder whether it was really so tough after all. The bus swung up in front of the Fort Harrison. At the door, as they descended, stood the trainer.

"All right now, you guys, everyone dressed for practice tomorrow at ten-thirty. Ten-thirty, remember." The Kid stepped out, surprised to find himself lame. Stiff and lame all over. Lame, but happy and content.

8

See, like this." Old Dave, the catcher, squatted down in front of the Kid's locker. "See, my right leg keeps the sign hidden from the first base coach, and the mitt, like this, screens it from the third base coach. All right. Now the only ones that can see it are you, the pitcher, and the shortstop . . . and of course a runner on second if there is one. Now when there's a runner on second, I use a switch signal. Unnerstand. . . ."

The Kid, seated on the bench before his locker with nothing on except his inner socks, nodded solemnly. He was dazed by the rapidity of it all. Two weeks before he had been in Clearwater, just another rookie about to be sent to the minors for a try-out; now he was seated in the dressing room at Ebbets Field in Brooklyn, ready for his first test in the big league. Even in a pre-season game no National League team had been able to trim the New York Yankees for some time, but the Dodgers, a last-place club the year before, had beaten them four out of six times in the exhibition games on the way north, and had taken two out of three in Brooklyn. So far the Kid hadn't been called on, but he was afraid he might be asked to go in for a few innings that afternoon. When Dave came across the room he was certain of it, and started pulling on his stockings to conceal his nerves. He rolled his trousers the way Dave had shown him in Florida so as to form a pad and give his knee bone the maximum protection in sliding to base.

"Now naturally I can't be sure the runner on second will nab that sign. He may, may not. If he does, he'll relay it to the coach and the batter, and you'll just be out of luck. I must be careful. I'm not taking any chances, see. So I give you the switch sign by touching my mask. Like this ... get me?"

The Kid swallowed hard. Yep, they were counting on throwing him in. Against the Yanks, too!

"Uhuh . . ." He pulled on his supporters. Then he put on a pair of heavy shorts, for he disliked the sliding pads some players wore, felt they restricted his movements. Dave continued.

"Now when I give you the switch signal, it means that one-finger-along-the-knee sign for a fast ball is really a curve, and the other way round. Get it? I hate like the dickens to change signs often, but you just have to change now and then. When a man leaves our club and goes to another club, for instance. I recall last year we had to change all our signals about five times in six weeks for various reasons. Now do you get that? Some boys don't seem to be able to remember signs at all, but you . . ."

"Oh, I getcha all right. But how about shaking you off?" he said, pulling on a white undershirt and sitting down on the bench to draw up his trousers.

"Well . . . use your judgment. Sometimes I like for pitchers to shake me off. Doesn't mean I'll always change the sign, mind you. Not at all; but I like to know my pitcher's doing some thinking out there for himself. If you feel in some particular case you can do better with a curve than the fast one I've called for, say so. Okay?"

The Kid nodded. He pulled on his shirt and leaned over to lace up his shoes, listening carefully all the while with his heart thumping as the older man continued. Yep, they were sure going to use him. . . .

". . . see, I just try to work with the pitcher, and take as much strain off him as possible. Remember I don't want you bothering about me; I want you to fix your attention on that-there guy at the plate. Two great things in a pitcher are control and confidence. Take old Fat Stuff over there; he hasn't got a very fast ball, but he has a change of pace and confidence. Also he's got a great big heart." Squatting on the floor he looked suddenly up as the Kid put a generous supply of chewing gum in his mouth. That glance went home.

"Getcha . . ." he nodded, chewing vigorously.

"Good. 'S I said just now, sometimes I like for a pitcher, especially a young pitcher, to shake me off. Y'see these hitters going against a kid like you, they're thinking about me all the time. They realize I know everything about them and their weaknesses; they know I know more than you do. Naturally, been round longer. . . . Oh,

DAVE SQUATTED DOWN IN FRONT OF THE KID

you'll pick it up, boy. Point is, when you shake me off the batter thinks I'm gonna switch. Only then I don't . . . see . . . I go back to the same sign and the hitter, not knowing this, is looking for something else. Chances are ten to one he'll only get a piece of the ball and not be able to hit it very good."

The Kid nodded and sat down, dressed and ready. Despite his nervousness he began to see the inside of baseball, began to realize its fascination and why it got men like old Fat Stuff who loved the game so much he wanted to stay on as an umpire after he was finished. The older man interrupted his thought by sitting beside him on the bench, wiping his forehead with his sleeve.

"Now these boys we're playing today. They're good batters, sure, but most every good batter has some weakness if you can only find it." The Kid's fright returned. If they were taking up the individual hitters it could only mean one thing. Gabby was pitching him for part of the game. "Take DiMag," continued the catcher. "Now when I was with the White Sox his first year we had a pitcher named Dietrich could get him out every time by pitching low. Fact. We got him every time for three games in a row, and then one day . . ."

"What'd he do then?"

The catcher laughed. "I hate to tell you. He got to a low ball and hit it into the back of the Yankee bullpen, longest hit I ever saw. When he comes up, well, keep 'em high and inside to him. And pray. He isn't hitting so good now anyhow. It's too early for him. Now then, this man Dickey. There's a dangerous batter. Keep it away and outside, and be sure you do. Rolfe? Well . . . a change of pace sometimes fools him badly. Let's try Gordon on a slow outside ball. If he connects during the game, why, we'll try something else. Baseball's a game of guessing; get me, you're in there trying hard to throw to their weakness, and the batter is in the box trying to outsmart you. And I'm helping, don't forget. . . . One thing more. If you get ahead, keep bearing down. This boy Nugent lets up, passes a couple of men as soon as he gets ahead, becomes careless and loses a game he oughta won. The boys don't like it. Keep bearing down all the time."

The Kid was nervous. There were little beads of sweat on his forehead as the catcher rolled those great names over casually: DiMag, Rolfe, Dickey; but despite his fear at the idea of facing the best team in baseball in his debut in the big leagues, that warm, friendly face and those smiling brown eyes reassured him. If he did go in, Dave would be there behind the plate, coaching, helping, pulling him along. There was a twinkle in those eyes which radiated confidence. It helped.

Then suddenly a door banged. Gabby entered, red-faced and perspiring from batting practice.

"Now then . . . you men . . ." he rasped. The room instantly became alert. By this time the Kid had learned some things about a big-league ballclub, and one was that not every man on the squad loved everybody else. Certainly Gabby was a slave-driver. But when he talked they listened.

"Last game now, you fellas. We beat those babies four times and Mac is awful anxious to sweep the Series today. I want you all in there scrapping, and I want plenty of holler . . . and bite, too. Remember you can't get a hit with your bats on your shoulders, and you can't get runs being nice boys out there on the bases. Jake, I want you and Rats and that kid, where is he, young Tucker . . . oh, there you are . . . I want you fellas to warm up. . . ."

The Kid felt as if everyone in the room was looking at him. Almost everyone was, too. Yep, he was going in. He flushed as faces turned his way, and hardly heard the last bitter-sharp words of their leader ending his charge.

". . . C'mon now, gang, some pepper out there. . . . Le's go. . . ."

Snatching their gloves from benches and lockers, the squad turned toward the door. Clack-clack, clackety-clack, clackety-clack, clack-clack their spikes sounded on the concrete runway leading from the dressing room to the field.

9

The crowd staggered him. It was a warm Saturday afternoon in mid-April, and a soft spring sunshine flooded the diamond. Ordinarily he would have been anxious to pitch, but the mob which jammed the lower stands, peered over from the second story, and even filled the bleachers in left center, was terrifying. He had never seen such a crowd before, and as he warmed up between Jake and Rats Doyle, he felt suddenly weak. The aisles even were full, and still more people were coming in every minute, and he could see them filling the boxes as he hurled his fast ball into that waiting mitt.

"Gosh, Rats, how many does this park hold? You know?"

Chewing energetically, the man beside him wound up, threw the ball, and grunted between his teeth. "Oh, this way it's close to capacity, I guess."

"How many is that?"

"Thirty thousand. Thirty-two maybe. With the deadheads. And if they fill those second story stands up there."

They were filling. Thirty thousand watching a game! The fans were in good humor too. They were shouting and calling out to Swanson, the center fielder, who had won the day before with a double in the ninth, they were yelling to Gabby Gus as he pranced round short, to Red Allen, the first baseman. But they seemed to be asking for something, for there was a note of insistence in the sound of their voices. A murmur ran round the stands, died away, and broke out again.

"Say . . . Rats . . . I'm sure glad I'm not starting today. Front of that gang . . ."

"What's the difference, boy? Crowds don't mean a thing. You'll get used to 'em soon enough. That's the trouble; then you'll get so you need 'em same as I do." He wound up and threw the ball. "Some guys hate it when the gang's out there, but me, I don't like to play to empty stands. This-here-now-crowd all steamed-up-like, makes me feel I wanna go."

Funny, thought the Kid. Imagine a man anxious to get out there against the Yanks in front of those packed stands. He felt heartily glad it wasn't his turn, for the crowd was still coming and there were still those queer insistent shouts from the bleachers.

"What's that yelling? What are they hollerin' about, Rats?"

"Them's the loyal rooters back of first. They want young Street to go in. They're hollering for Gabby to shove Street in . . . at that he might let the boy have a few innings today."

A sudden panicky feeling ran up and down the Kid's spine. Maybe he'd shove me in. No, unlikely, because it was Jake's turn to pitch, and besides, the veteran was always effective against the Yanks. Then the bell clanged and the Dodger fielders rose from the dugout to take the diamond as the three pitchers walked in. Gabby came toward them.

"Whaddya say, Tuck old boy? 'Bout ready?"

"Who? Me? You want me . . . want me to start in there, Gabby?" He looked for Jake, but his waddling form was nearing the dugout, pulling on his jacket, his chunky legs churning the ground, his huge arms swinging outwards. Jake must have known all the time. The Kid was seized with a terrible fright; why, he'd make a fool of himself. He'd be a joke out...

"Sure, I want you in there. Remember this is just an exhibition. Get out and do your best; never mind the crowd. They're pulling for you hard."

He yanked his glove desperately from his hip pocket and started toward the box. Someone slapped him hard on the back and ran past into the field . . . Harry Street! Harry was playing short in place of Gabby. A roar greeted him as he neared the mound, for the fans were anxious to see him even if he wasn't anxious to see them. Nervous, timid, uncertain, he rubbed the ball in his hands and threw it. Old Leonard stood smiling behind the plate. The first ball was high and wide, but the second burned across into his mitt, and the old catcher grinned as he tossed it back. The Kid put more into the next and the next. Now his confidence was returning. Leonard nodded; he nodded back....

MacManus was tired. He had flown out to

Kansas City to see a young third baseman play, jumped another plane to Nashville the same night for a conference with his farm manager, taken the air again to return to New York, been grounded in Pittsburgh in a storm, and reached Brooklyn by train early that morning. But no one would have guessed he was tired. Apparently he had as much vitality as ever, sitting behind his desk attending to a hundred details; now leaning back in his chair and tossing his horn-rimmed glasses on the desk, now yanking his feet back suddenly to the floor, pressing the buzzer, reaching for the telephone, banging it down, and pounding his fist into his palm to emphasize a point he was making to the visitor in front. Seated with him was Jim Casey who after a few innings of the game had dropped into the office to watch the fiery owner's reaction to the latest insult of his rival, the Giant manager.

"No, I haven't seen a paper. We were grounded in Pittsburgh yesterday by that storm, and I took a train, so I was late getting in and haven't had a chance to look at the sports news. What's more, I've got nothing to say . . . nothing. . . ."

But Casey knew his man. He continued as if he hadn't heard the last remark. "Murphy was sounding off yesterday when he heard you won that game against the Yanks in the tenth. Said he guessed the Dodgers must be pretty good. Said the team that beats Brooklyn will win the pennant this year."

A flush of red came over the other's face. He half rose, leaning over toward the sportswriter and pounding the table. "Why . . . . why, that big . . . why, the big bum . . . the Giants . . . Say, those guys will be lucky to keep ahead of Philadelphia. And you can say I said so too. . . . Lemme tell you something. . . ." The telephone interrupted him. It was a long conversation and when he had finished, the sportswriter changed the subject. He had just what he'd come for.

"Seems to me, Jack, like this fogger out there might turn into something. He seems to have pretty good control for a rookie."

"Yeah . . . yeah, he may be a ballplayer in a couple of years. Know how I happened to land him, don't you? You don't? I was up there in Waterbury after Simpson, their shortstop, and this here kid from some hick town was in pitching. He pitched six innings and that was enough for me. I says to their manager, I said . . . Excuse me . . ." The telephone jangled again. "Yeah, I'll talk . . . put him on. . . . Hullo, Hank . . . Sure. How you? Pretty good, thanks. . . . Well, we got a hustlin' ballclub; tha's more than we had last summer. No, can't say much more right now. What's that? No, I haven't heard Murphy's last crack, and what's more . . . he says . . . What? . . . If we play night baseball . . . He did, hey? . . . Well, you get this straight. . . . Just say we started night baseball; so let him stop popping off about us and mind his own business. That's all. We'll look out after ourselves. G'by. . . ." He slammed the telephone back on the little table at one side, a table ornamented by three different receivers. "Murphy! Popping off again. Says the Dodgers may finish in the second division if they play enough at night 'cause no one else can see the ball. Say, you know that guy gives me a pain in the neck. Well, I was telling you about this lad Tucker. He sure is one hustling ballplayer and don't you forget it either. One day at Clearwater I came down early to practice and he was all dressed and out with Charlie Draper and a couple of the boys. I heard 'em talking. Charlie was hitting fungoes to 'em, and pretty soon this kid pipes up. 'Man, you can't hit fungoes. Lemme hit the ball myself.' Yessir, it's a fact; he picks up the bat, hits a fungo, and then runs out into the field, catches it. For half an hour. How's that for spirit? I wish we had twenty men on the team with pep like that." The telephone buzzed again.

"Uhuh . . . put him on. . . . Hello, Tom . . . he did . . . it is . . . okay . . . keep me posted. . . ." There was a roar from outside which penetrated the quiet little room. "Fine. Good. Well, I think he ought to stay in; give him confidence, and that's what he needs most of all. But Gabby'll have to use his own judgment." He slammed back the telephone and turned with a satisfied grin to the visitor. "Nothing to nothing, end of the fifth, and the Yanks haven't had a man on second yet. . . ."

Out on the field the Kid hardly knew what to do. If he didn't tip his cap it might look fatheaded, but then it might be that stop of Red Allen's, the first out of the inning, or the line drive back of second Harry nabbed. He couldn't tell what they were yelling about, but as he crossed the first base line toward the dugout he knew they were cheering his pitching, so he touched his cap awkwardly and hurried in as fast as he could. All up and down the long bench came warm-hearted words, often from friends and often also from men who were trying for the same position, who saw themselves shunted off to the minors or even out of a job if he kept on as he was going. Nevertheless they meant what they said.

"Thassa way to pour it in, Roy old boy. . . ."

"That's throwing that old tomato, Roy. . . ."

"Now you're showing those big stiffs something, Kid. That's the way to chuck 'em." And Doc Masters, who three weeks before at Clearwater had hardly noticed a bad blister which prevented him from running, now jumped up quickly and came over where he was sitting. Squeezing in unceremoniously, he started massaging his arm and asking how he felt.

"You're up after Swanson, Tuck," called someone. He reached for his favorite bat when a roar rose from the stands. It was a long clean hit deep into center field and all three fielders were scurrying for it as the batter, head down, rounded first and started for second. The roar changed into a groan, followed by applause. The New York fielder had nabbed the ball out by the fence, shutting out a sure three-base hit.

"He certainly can pound that old pea," someone behind him remarked. Disgusted, the batter came back to the dugout and as he passed the Kid:

"Nuts . . . That was robbery. . . ."

The Kid walked up to the plate. There was some scattered applause as he stood facing the man in the box. From behind in the dugout and on the coaching lines came calls for a hit. He yanked his cap down over his eyes and waited. The first ball caught the outer edge . . . a strike.

Cries of derision came across the infield as, face flushed, he stood watching the motionless man on the mound. This one he'd hit. If it was any good at all he'd clout it . . . he'd . . .

Nearing first he caught Charlie Draper waving him frantically on, and he came into second standing up, rounded the base, and started for third when he saw Gabby on the coaching lines yelling him back. Digging in his spikes he slid to a stop, turned, and retreated toward second. The ball came swift and low to third, and he would have been out even with the best of slides. Standing triumphantly on second, he watched the pitcher and catcher consulting between home and the box, their heads together. That was the same pitcher, he reflected, who had won two World Series games the previous fall.

The crowd was standing to yell and the noise warmed him all over. Now they'd have to keep him. They couldn't send him to Nashville or some farm team now. His mind went back a month when, lonesome and homesick, he looked forward to a chance with Nashville as the greatest possible success to be obtained. Today Nashville would have seemed failure. Funny how a few weeks changed the picture. Back of Gabby on the coaching lines three photographers were kneeling to catch him as he rounded third for the plate, to snap him, the Kid from Tomkinsville who shut out the mighty Yanks for six, seven, innings it was, without a hit. He turned to glance at the scoreboard and the string of zeros beside the word VISITORS. Nothing to nothing, the end of the seventh, and Karl Case, a good steady hitter, at bat. This might well be the

IF IT WAS ANY GOOD AT ALL, HE'D CLOUT IT

winning run. Never had he felt surer, never more confident, and instead of tiring as the game went on he was so completely master of the ball, he knew he could pitch all afternoon that way if only Dave Leonard stood there, steady and helpful at the other end.

Case was waiting. The Kid returned to life, danced off the bag, watched the pitcher turn and eye him, darted back as the shortstop veered toward the bag. Two balls. A walk. One strike. Three balls. Case flung his bat toward the dugout and started for first. Now Red Allen approached the plate swinging the bat in his hands. Now, he thought, be ready; Red will hit it. But all the time in the back of his mind was the one big thought: shut them out, shut them out, shut them out. . . .

Bang. The whole field was running. Everyone was running and everyone was shouting. Hang it, he was on his heels when he should have been on his toes, for it was a hit to deep left center and the Yankee fielders were after it. The Kid dug in his spikes, feeling sure he would score, when suddenly as he rounded third an enormous yell came to him. Roscoe, the man who caught that first hit, had made another impossible catch; their rally was cut off and that one run lead which looked so big was still to be made. The inning was over, so he slowed down, stopping to save his energy as Dave had taught him, and turning watched the fielder shoot in the ball to the infield. Then there was a queer shout . . . two or three yells; the second baseman was standing with his arms open on the base, the ball coming in from the field, Gabby with an angry expression....

Big Bill Hanson, the business manager, burst into the room where MacManus and the sports-writer were together. He was excited and out of breath as he talked, and the man behind the desk yanked his feet to the floor with a jerk.

"The devil you say...."

"Yeah; well, that's how it is with rookies. Shutting out the Yankees, let's see now, seven innings straight, was too much I guess. He must have been dreaming himself into the World Series or something. Say, I never hope to see a man as mad as Gabby. He swears he yelled 'Two out! Get back, get back,' right in the boy's face. Says the Kid turned and looked at the scoreboard only a moment before and must have seen there was only one out. Gabby sure was fit to be tied. 'You big useless busher,' he shouted. 'Don't you know yet how many outs in a baseball game?' And you should have seen the Kid's face. Point was he could have made third easy enough, and with Kennedy up most likely he would have scored. The way he was going those Yanks would have been out there waving their bats until to-morrow morning."

"That's Yankee luck. Too bad he had to be taken out. Well, Gabby knows his stuff."

"Gabby yanked him quick as quick, and when he got back to the bench slapped a fifty dollar fine on him. The poor boob was so flustered he didn't know what to say or how to take it, and the gang, half of 'em wanted to laugh and the other half felt kinda sorry for the boy. Then

Jake went in and they got out their bats and started hitting him all over the park. Seven to nothing now. Gabby got madder'n ever."

"Dumb work all right. Well, rookies are like that. You have to play an awful long while and make a lot of mistakes before you know anything. Don't worry. I'd like to have copped that game, but we can't win 'em all. They might have hit him the next inning same as Jake, how do you know?" The telephone tinkled. "Who? . . . Yeah, I'll talk. . . . Hullo there, Mac. . . . How are you?"

10

The kid got the news the afternoon of their first night game about six weeks after the season opened. The Dodgers were in second place, only a game behind the Cincinnati Reds whom they were playing that evening, when he met Razzle Nugent in the lobby of the St. George where the team lived in Brooklyn.

"Hey there, Roy . . . heard the latest?" Razzle enjoyed a sensation. He appreciated that the Kid would be rocked by latest developments in the club office and was anxious to see the effect. "They're letting out old Leonard tomorrow."

The Kid stopped. Dave leaving the team! Impossible! "Yep, that's right. Case heard it from the business manager at lunch this noon." But this was disaster. How would he be able to pitch without those steadying brown eyes from behind the plate? Maybe it wasn't true. Maybe it was only one of Razzle's jokes; Razzle was always kidding. But all the time in his heart the Kid knew it wasn't a joke, at least as far as he was concerned.

"Are you sure, Razzle? Did he tell you? . . ."

"Ask Gabby Spencer. Here he comes." The manager came across the lobby with quick, nervous steps.

"Hey, boys! Tuck, you know it's your turn to go in, don't you? And we want this game the worst way, too."

"Tonight?" His first game at night. And without Dave back of the plate. In desperation he spoke up. "Don't suppose, Gabby, you could let Dave catch me tonight, could you? I'd pitch better ball, I think."

The manager started to shake his head, looked at him with clouded face. "I'd much rather have Stansworth catch you. That's what I planned. You gotta get used to him; y'see, it's time to cut the squad, and we had to let old Leonard out." Then, watching the disappointment and despair in his expression, "Well, if Dave wants to go in, it's okay with me. We must win this game, that's all."

The Kid took the elevator to the fourteenth floor, but there was no reply to his knock on Dave's door. However, the veteran catcher was taking off his clothes when he reached the ball park that evening, and grinned across the lighted dressing room as though nothing had happened, although by this time the Kid knew enough about his home and his life to realize that plenty had happened. Silently the Kid took his shirt, trousers, and underwear from the locker and began to dress. All at once it struck him.

The last time! The last time he'll ever catch me! The suddenness with which it had happened was terrifying; one minute Dave was Leonard, the veteran catcher to whom everyone on the squad came for help and advice; the next minute he was out. Given his release. It was like his own climb in a few months as an unknown rookie from a small Connecticut town to a celebrated figure in big-time baseball with his name on the sports pages of every metropolitan daily. The Kid, the Kid from Tomkinsville . . . that star rookie the Dodgers picked up last spring. . . .

Speed, he reflected as he took off his clothes and drew on his uniform, speed was what counted in baseball. Well, here was a speed they didn't often mention: the speed with which a player rises—and goes down. Speed? Yep, there was speed for you. No more Dave behind the plate. Why, he couldn't pitch to those other mugs! He'd tried it often; it didn't work. Dave was *his* catcher. It was Dave who'd taught him all he knew, showed him the apparently simple but difficult knack of steering his number two pitch down the proper channel, neither too high where the batter could knock it a mile nor yet too low where even Dave, his best friend, couldn't reach it.

What would he do without Dave quietly squatting on his hams, down in the crouch until the ball came? The other catchers always rose as he threw the ball. Besides giving him no target at which to throw, this motion frequently caught his eye and distracted him. There just wasn't anyone like Dave. Anyone to kill that nightmare of all pitchers, the hit-and-run. Other catchers let opposing teams get away with it and blamed him as a rookie. Suspecting a hit-and-run, the catcher calls for a pitch-out even on the two-and-

nothing pitch. But in calling for such a pitch most catchers betrayed themselves by leaping from the box to catch the ball, so runners were invariably tipped off. Dave never did this. He was too smart a catcher, he always waited that extra second, that dangerous second, and nabbed the runner on bases. It was those little things which made Dave different, which helped and steadied a young pitcher in critical moments of close games. He needed Dave. He had to have

Dave. Stuffing in his shirt and buckling the belt of his trousers he wandered across to the old catcher, hardly knowing what to say.

"Gosh, Dave, what'm I gonna do now?"

"Do? Go in there tonight and win that ball game. Pitch your head off, boy; that's what you're going to do. We have to have this game." His arm in the Kid's, he drew him outside and through the ramp onto the field. And the Kid resolved that for Dave it would be the best game he ever pitched.

Batting practice was held in the setting sun, while two bands entertained the early comers. Already the stands were filling up and it was plain a crowd would be on hand at game-time. Daylight lasted until almost eight-thirty, and in between batting practice there were stunts to amuse the bleachers, a footrace in which Jess Owens, the colored Olympic sprinter, ran a foot-race against Harry Street, the fastest man on the team, giving him a ten-yard start in a hundred yards. Going back to the bench for a minute the Kid heard someone say, "Fire department just ordered the gates closed. Bet Mac is happy; look at that gang coming in." He glanced up at the stands. They were almost filled but still the crowd was pouring through the entrances.

By the time Dave stepped out to warm him up, dusk had settled over the field and there were rockets and flares and fireworks to add to the excitement. Even in deep center he could see the boxes and upper stands filling, which meant a capacity crowd. Soon the powerful arc lights on the roof went on, the stands roaring approval. They made the field emerald green and their uniforms glistening white. There wasn't a vacant spot visible.

Rats Doyle, warming up beside him, said between pitches, "Jack says they've turned about ten thousand away already. Look at that mob out there in left center." The crowd had packed the seats and was standing in the aisles. Meanwhile the loudspeaker was issuing statistics on the power of illumination.

". . . sitting on second base and reading a newspaper would have ten times as much light as necessary. . . . These lights would illuminate a highway 447 miles long, or a town of 2,000 city blocks. . . ." Dave beckoned him in to the bench. The loudspeaker was giving the batting order. ". . . shortstop . . . catcher, No. 38, Leonard . . . pitcher, No. 56, Tucker. For Cincinnati . . ." But his words were drowned in an enormous yell. The fans had come to see the Kid pitch them into first place, and this made him more nervous because he wanted it to be the best game he'd ever pitched. With difficulty he heard Dave beside him on the bench quietly speaking in his ear, a ball moving up and down in his right hand:

"Whatever you do, Roy, don't tighten up. Just forget the team is up there in second place. Imagine you were down in Florida again; don't pay attention to that gang there. Remember this is just another game, that's all, and pitch like it was. Now come on out." A roar, the mightiest roar he'd ever heard, smacked him in the face as he walked slowly out to the box in the middle of that emerald-green floor. Everything seemed false and unreal—the strange light, the tremendous crowd, the night wind on his face, the queer look from behind Dave's mask; he was in a daze, hardly knowing what he was doing. Mechanically he loosened his muscles, threw the ball as directed, and then heard the crowd shout when Swanson in center pulled down an easy fly for the first out. The next man was hard to pitch to and got a base on balls. This brought another roar, for there were plenty of Brooklyn fans ready to see the Dodgers lose.

He was rattled. He knew he was rattled. Maybe it was the tense atmosphere in the park, inevitable when two teams separated only by a single game were struggling for the lead, or perhaps that eerie feeling caused by the unnaturalness of his surroundings, the cool night wind, and those lights flaring from both sides of the roof. Maybe it was the noisy crowd, or the coming departure of his friend, the man who had pushed and pulled him from a nameless rookie to a winning pitcher on a pennant contender. He didn't know, couldn't tell; he only knew his delivery was stiff and strained, and that there was no looseness in his motion. Now Rosetti, the leading batter in the League and the star left fielder of the Cincinnati nine, came to the plate as the stands shouted advice from above. Could he fail on Dave's last time behind the bat, the one time he wanted above all to do his best!

No. Not that. Putting everything into his first pitch, a curve on the outer edge, he watched Rosetti step in and catch it on the nose. The ball sizzled past before he could recover balance, a clean hit which meant at least one run. Then something happened. It was that something which was making this group of men pennant contenders, keeping them on top in the race. The Kid had seen the play a thousand times, never better performed than at that moment.

From out of nowhere came little Eddie Davis, the second baseman, running full tilt, his body over, his glove outstretched as the ball skinned the ground. There was a gasp round the stands when he stopped it with one hand and without straightening or regaining balance tossed it to Gabby on a string. The ball was shoulder high, and he caught it without any shift in his stride.

Gabby was five feet from the bag when he picked the ball out of the air. Quick as a cat he crossed the bag and losing not a fraction of a second whipped it to Allen at first. Back of second one umpire's hand went into the air; beside first the hand of the other umpire rose, and with it a full-throated roar from the crowd. The Kid stood watching, helpless and fascinated, seeing the three men function in unison, every reflex, every muscle, attuned to a job where the slightest delay, the slightest misstep or error in timing, would mean failure. There was the perfect co-ordination of arms and legs, there was the perfect fielding and throwing necessary to get Spike Rosetti, one of the fastest men in baseball, by a step and a half at first. Something came into his throat, he half choked, and then the confidence which had been missing all evening swept over him. There . . . how could any pitcher lose with men like that behind him!

The roars still rung in his ears when he rolled the thumb of his glove and stuffed it into his hip pocket, coming toward the bench. He heard Gabby's words through a haze. "Let's get some runs, gang. . . ." Squeezing into his place in the dugout he felt again that surge of confidence and knew he'd pitch ball the rest of the game. On the mound again he saw this was true. He had everything. The batters were little boys and he was playing with them; obeying Dave's orders he stood watching them hit weak pop-ups or lazy grounders to the infield. In fact it wasn't until well along in the game, until about the fifth inning, that the chance for a no-hit game occurred to him. The Kid wasn't pitching only for himself, he was pitching for the team and most of all for Dave. Dave's last game was going to be one they'd never forget.

Those who lived it never would forget it either. Already Allen and Case and Swanson had given him a run which looked as big as a hundred the way he was going. Interest round the field now centered in the Kid's chances for a no-hit game, and already a low murmur rose as the stands saw inning after inning go past without a hit from the visiting club. On the bench everyone realized it too, but everyone kept discreetly quiet on account of the Whammy. Mustn't put the Whammy on him! Gabby chattered about the lights and the yellow ball, Case said as far as he was concerned he'd much rather play all games at night, and Swanson in center remarked that nowadays a guy was playing the moonfield and not the sunfield, at which everyone chuckled in kind of a grim way. Because everyone felt the strain. And when the team was batting, the Kid sat on the bench beside Dave with the older

man's hand on his knee, as the sixth went into the seventh and the fans rose to stretch for the Dodgers, and the seventh became the eighth, and the eighth went into the ninth with no hits, and not a man on base since the fumbling, bungling inning at the start of the game.

The stands rose in a kind of frenzy as he came out to take the box in the beginning of the ninth. Here was baseball history and they were in at the kill. There was a continual roar all around the diamond, and the whole crowd was on their feet. Even from deep center he could hear the roar and the shouts of encouragement, for now the fans were behind him to a man. Three runners out and they'd lead the League! Three putouts and he'd have a no-hit game! He, Roy Tucker, the Kid from Tomkinsville would have...

He walked across in that feverish atmosphere to the box. There he took the ball, straightened out the stepping holes made by Thompson, the Reds' pitcher, and, stuffing down his shirt, hitched up his pants. Taking a couple of pitches, he faced the batter. His first was a ball. He stood hardly hearing the steady roar from the stands.

"Ball two . . ." called old Sourpuss Kiggins, the umpire, behind the plate. His voice brought the Kid back quickly to the shrieking ball park, to Dave calmly kneeling back of the batter, to the Cincinnati coaches shouting for a hit from the coaching boxes. He burned in his fast one and a roar greeted him as the umpire raised his hand and pointed toward the right. But the next pitch was a ball. Three and one.

Crack! The ball was in the air. Back, Dave, back. . . . Roy saw his agonized face searching the sky through that daze of blinding lights, watched him run behind third, heard the shouts. "Leonard . . . Leonard . . . yours, Dave. . . ." The catcher stumbled momentarily over a glove, caught himself, got to the boxes, leaned over . . . and caught the ball in his outstretched mitt. Again that mighty roar sweeping the entire park. One down. Only two more men to go!

The noise increased. Out in left center they were throwing torn paper onto the field. Now Hartwick, the Cincinnati shortstop, came to the plate swinging two bats in a confident manner. As the record approached, the Kid's confidence which had kept him up ever since the first inning wavered. Suppose he let them hit it? Those two batters became an impossible obstacle, and his poise and assurance faltered. With it went his control and Hartwick was trotting down to first.

When Dave snapped the ball back, he saw Gabby from one corner of his eye shout something between cupped hands. What was it? The Kid never knew, but it hardly helped settle him, and again he found difficulty locating the plate. Vainly the catcher called for a curve, for that favorite fast ball shoulder high, for a low ball hopping by the knees. He couldn't. For some strange reason his magic touch vanished. Carey, the Cincinnati batter, slung away his bat and moved to first while the crowd shrieked. They wanted a no-hit game.

"Ball one!" The coaches on the lines were calling above the noise, clapping their hands eagerly. At last he was blowing. Stockton, the Red clean-up man, eager to hit the ball but still more anxious to prove by the third base on balls that the pitcher was going to pieces, stood crowding the plate. The Kid tried to shoot one close in; the batter half turned to avoid the ball and it caught him on the elbow. Rubbing his arm furiously he slung away his bat, while the umpire motioned him to first. Three men on. Anything beyond the infield meant a score. The winning run on second!

The crowd was mad. From the bench and from his mates in the field behind him came half-hearted shouts of encouragement, from the stands the cries of an insane mob. In that frenzied atmosphere only one man was collected, the sturdy, brown-eyed figure in the mask. He walked slowly down the path, exactly the same as that morning in Clearwater when he came toward the Kid saying: "Show me how you hold that ball." If Dave was disturbed or upset by the situation, he didn't betray the least emotion. Instead he came toward the box, closer and closer, while the three Cincinnati runners stood perched on each base, and the roars grew in volume.

"Listen, Kid." He had to lean close to make himself heard. "Listen . . . those hitters are more scared of you than you are of them. Don't forget it. Jest pour that old ball in where I tell you."

It was exactly what Roy needed. Forgetting the dancing runners, arms outstretched on the basepaths, he concentrated on the batter. Workman, the catcher and a dangerous man, was at the plate. Dave smiled and went into his crouch.

The signal came for a fast one, and the Kid burned the ball down the middle.

"Strike . . . one. . . ." The last word was lost in the tumult.

He glanced about to see his infield playing deep, looked over his shoulder, and then, getting the signal, nodded. Dave would pull him through. Old Dave who knew every hitter and the weakness of every hitter in the League would get him out of this spot. Close . . . inside. He wound up quickly, and the hitter swung violently as the ball plunked with that full comforting sound into Dave's mitt. Again the air resounded. And the ball came swiftly back at him.

Two and nothing. Wasting one pitch, he burned the next one over low and inside. The batter caught it with the end of his bat, and tapped it weakly toward third. Jerry came running in, scooped it, and hurled it swift and low at the plate. Touch and go . . . the man was forced out. Had Dave needed to tag him he might have slid safely, but now there were two down and again frenzy took possession of the crowd. One putout from first place. One putout from a no-hit game!

It was Drake, the big first baseman. Not a .300 hitter and not a bad one either; a chap who batted in lots of runs. Before the game they'd agreed to keep the ball low to Drake, but the first pitch was too low. Ball one. As he turned back to the box he noticed the big clock in right field pointed to ten past eleven. In a few minutes, in two-three minutes, it would all be over; they'd have won or lost and he'd be in the showers, cooling his aching muscles, refreshing his pounding head. Only two minutes, only a few pitches more, only a bit longer now. He took the signal, the same low ball, looked round, wound up and let go. "Ball two!" The roar rose, a sea of noise echoing against the bleachers, bouncing back against the packed stands behind the plate, echoing outside the ball park. Two and none. Only two balls from danger. Possibly from defeat. Be careful now. Don't take chances. Play safe . . . get that batter. He nodded at Dave, looked carefully round at the dancing trio on the basepaths, wound up quickly, and shot in his curve. The batter swung over it as the roar deepened. Two and one.

While he stood scuffing the dirt and shoving his shirt back into his pants, the crowd was shrieking its desire for those last two balls, the balls which would mean the end of the game. The suspense was more than they could stand. Only two strikes. Two strikes, that's all. Dear God . . . two strikes—give me two strikes . . . just two strikes . . . two strikes and . . .

From the box he watched Dave, still the same unworried, unhurried Dave, go into his crouch. No, not that. Not the fast one. Too risky. He didn't dare; he was too frightened to try it. So he shook Dave off. But the catcher insisted, and insisted with such energy that all at once the Kid remembered. This was Dave's trick. The batter would think they were switching when they weren't.

At the plate the big Cincinnati first basemen stood menacingly swinging his bat and crowding the plate. That pitcher was scared. Ah, that rookie was frightened. This was the cripple; this was the one to hit. He stood ready, waiting, and as the ball came down the groove swung a trifle late.

The ball went up in the air.

The second he swung the Kid knew he was late, but his heart thumped. Then he realized it was up in the air. Behind him someone was going back, Gabby and Jerry Strong, the third baseman, together, while Tommy Scudder in left was racing in toward them. Even through the noise he could hear Gabby's piercing yell.

"MINE . . . MINE . . . MINE. . . ."

The Kid started to run for the dugout because he knew they'd mob him. Actually he started running as the ball settled into Gabby's hands, but his teammates were too quick. They made him a prisoner, clumped him on the back, wrung his tired right hand till it was limp and sore. By the time they reached the exit his feet were off the ground, and the crowd leaning over poked him on the back, touched his arm, his sleeve, his body, showered bits of torn paper down, yelled and cheered. In the dressing room it was worse.

Just inside the door stood MacManus with his Irish grin and a hand that almost wrenched the Kid's off. Doc Masters was slapping everyone with a towel, and old Chiselbeak, who looked after their clothes and did the locker room chores, was handing out Cokes with abandon. Excited shouts, laughter, general pandemonium, the door opening every second to let in some sportswriter, Casey with his hat off and a cigarette in his mouth as excited as the rest. Through it all the Kid was neither too stirred nor too happy to forget the man who made all this possible. He struggled through the gang and fought his way across the room to the catcher's locker. Sweaty, tired, lines of fatigue under his eyes betraying the strain of the evening, Dave was pulling off his Brooklyn uniform. For the last time.

Maybe not. Maybe it wasn't the last time after all. The Kid pushed through, but others were already beside him. From the stands it was Roy Tucker, the young rookie, the new Dodger star; but the men who had watched from the field and seen Dave carry him through the game and then pull his pitcher together in the tense moments of the ninth to outguess the best hitting team in baseball, they knew. He felt warm and pleased as he watched them patting Dave's back, grabbing his fist, calling through cupped hands in the noise and pandemonium. He tried to catch Gabby's eye. Was Gabby noticing this too? Maybe it would make a difference, maybe Gabby would change his mind. Gabby knew baseball, Gabby did.

No, Gabby wouldn't change his mind. Because this was life, baseball was, and life was like that. One minute you were unknown and the next minute you were up in front; one minute you were a fixture on a club and then the next out of a job. Before his locker, Dave was pulling off a wet shirt with the word Dodgers on it. For the last time.

11

The kid missed him badly. With Dave gone there was no one to turn to for advice, no one who could help when he had new batters to face, nobody to whose room he could go in the evening when he felt on the spot as his winning record grew each time he took the box. And with his record, the strain. Because now everyone knew about the Kid from Tomkinsville. Fans in other towns poured out merely to see whether he'd add another game to his winning list, and opposing teams invariably put more punch into their attack in the hopes of breaking the spell.

The strain was general. The whole squad felt it. With the team in first place by half a game one day and trailing the Cincinnati Reds by a game the next day, every pitch, every throw to first, every catch in the outfield, was vital. Moreover the break between the first and second division became sharper as New York, goaded on by Murphy, and Chicago, with good-natured Earl Bartlett, their catcher and manager, pulling them along, came closer and closer. Gabby was like a mechanical toy wound up and unable to stop.

FANS POURED OUT TO SEE HIM AND GET HIS AUTOGRAPH

Each afternoon he was on the basepaths scrapping with the enemy players and umpires alike, a very comforting person for the Kid to have behind him during a close game. There was the series in Chicago, for instance, which wound up with both teams raising their spikes and the pitcher dusting off the hitters as if they were in there for that one purpose. Buzzy Adams, the big Chicago ace, was noted for loosening up the batters, and he took it out on the Dodgers so that even the best hitters on the squad began going into the bucket. Gabby decided something must be done. When he came to bat early in the game he deliberately got on Adams.

"Get your feet off the plate, Gabby," cautioned the big man in the box. Gabby, like a terrier, shook himself with rage.

"Why, Buzzy, you haven't got guts enough to dust me off," he said, pounding the plate with his bat and scowling.

A minute later a fast ball scraped his chin.

"Try that again and I'll knock your block off. . . ." He picked up his bat which had fallen from his hands as he ducked back, and stood in silence at the plate, waiting, with everyone in the stands and on the two teams watching the duel of nerves between the pitcher and batter. Gabby crowded the plate a bit closer, while the coaching lines rang with angry yells from Draper and Cassidy, the first base coach. Buz wound up slowly, and the ball came. . . .

"Ball twooo . . ." It was wide and outside. The count ran to three and two and then Gabby got his base on balls. For some reason Buzzy kept his pitches away from them the rest of the game.

Sometimes, however, Gabby's tight nerves and scrappy spirit affected the morale of the club. In St. Louis one afternoon in a close game there were men on first and second with none out and the score two to nothing against the Dodgers. From the bench Gabby gave Swanson the signal for a bunt. The pitcher threw two wild ones, and on the next pitch Swanson hit a "gopher ball" out of the park. Those three runs put them ahead, and eventually won the game. While half the team swarmed from the dugout to shake the center fielder's hand, Gabby stormed to the plate, raging.

"Get in to the clubhouse, you fathead," he shouted. No one saw Swanson the rest of the afternoon, or Gabby either, because he took himself out and spent the time lecturing Swanny on the value of discipline. To make it sink in, he finished by slapping on a $50 fine. Two days later when Big Bill McLoughlin, the Cardinal catcher, hit a home run, Gabby fined Swanson $25 more for failing to hustle after the hit. Everyone wondered where and when Gabby's explosive temper would strike next.

Meanwhile the team was partly crippled by injuries of the usual sort. A fighting ballclub means a club that takes chances, and taking chances inevitably brings on minor injuries and bruises; a lame back here, a weakened ankle there, a sore arm or a bad shoulder. Many of them carried "strawberries," those painful patches of raw skin as big as a football that come on players' hips and legs from sliding. Red Allen and Karl Case were in batting slumps which didn't help. Only the hurlers continued to hold up, with

Roy the number one and Razzle Nugent the number two man close behind. The pitching staff was turning in pennant-winning stuff.

They came into Pittsburgh in first place, a game and a half ahead of Cincinnati and three games ahead of the third-place Cubs. Gabby had a routine with his pitchers that seemed to work. He explained it to Roy. On some teams pitchers frequently got a day off after a full game, but with Gabby never.

"A pitcher should do something to exercise his arm every afternoon, and especially on resting day. You pitched yesterday. Jake goes in day after tomorrow. All right. I want you out there warming up that arm this afternoon. That removes any kinks or sore spots that might have set in overnight. Jake will throw part of batting practice today, and Rats and Fat Stuff too. Tomorrow Frenchie De Voe goes in, and Jake rests, while you and Rats take batting practice. Jake goes in Thursday and you can rest that day. Y'see, some boys need more arm exercise than others, but everyone ought to tune up between starts."

The system worked. Razzle threw a great game that afternoon, shutting Pittsburgh out with only three hits, and Gabby, feeling his pitcher needed some relaxing, told him to have a couple of beers, Razzle's favorite drink, with his dinner. Although their victory was hurt by the misfortune to Jerry Strong, the third baseman, who was lost for a while. A Pittsburgh batter on first tried to stretch a single to right. Furious that Karl Case's throw was there waiting for him, he carved his initials into Jerry's legs and the little third baseman had to be carried off the field. Right on top of that came another disaster.

The Kid was lying on his bed after dinner in his room in the Schenley across from Forbes Field, where the Dodgers always stayed in Pittsburgh. He was reading Casey's column in the *Post-Gazette*. Now Casey's column was the sort of thing you always chuckled over when Casey talked about someone else or some other team. That evening the Kid enjoyed it. For Casey was exercising his wit at the expense of the Chicago management, gentlemen with whom he had never seen eye to eye.

"Frederick Charles Robertson was the baby they were all hollering about down South last spring in the training camps. Maybe you remember. He came from the Pacific Coast League where he was a sensation, to join the Chicago Cubs, who paid plenty for him. $100,000 was the figure, and never denied. All through spring training Mr. Robertson got the headlines. He was a feature story for every touring baseball writer. One of the big national weeklies gave him an elaborate spread. It was young Robertson this, and young Robertson that.

"All the while a youth named Roy Tucker was working out quietly with the Brooklyn Dodgers at Clearwater. It seems this lad had no money to report to the team, so he borrowed carfare from his grandmother with whom he lives on a farm outside Tomkinsville, Connecticut. Going through the routine without benefit of headlines, he was just another rookie that Jack MacManus had picked up somewhere. One more of Wild Jack's mistakes, the boys explained.

"None of the touring scribes stopped to interview Roy. None of the national weeklies played him up. He was merely one more freshman in training camps. A good-looking kid who might do for a season with Decatur. Well, here it is almost August, and what about it? That unknown kid from Tomkinsville is about the hottest thing in pitching in either league. He started winning in May and hasn't stopped yet. Everyone knows his record and how the other night over in Cincinnati he shut out the league-leading Reds without a hit."

The Kid's face grew hotter and hotter. Gosh! Why, Casey wasn't such a bad guy after all! Why did all the players pan Casey, and keep away from him so much? He must be all right, that man Casey. The printed page danced before his eyes.

" 'Tucker wins again,' sing the headlines. He's copped his fourteenth straight victory, the best record any first-year pitcher ever made. He's a fogger with a fast one that's fast, a curve that breaks, and he pitches with his noodle. He knows how to play the hitter and what to do with the ball. He'll take advice, and the boys say he will get better as he goes along, and incidentally he can pound that pill, too. Several games he's won by timely hits at the right moment. He's as fast as anyone on the club, he can field, and if he could cook I'd marry him."

Yessir, Casey was all right. He'd stand up for Casey when the boys started panning him at table and saying these newspaper bums didn't know anything about baseball. He sure would stand up for him. Casey was a great person. Understood the game, too. You could tell that just by reading him. He continued.

"And Robertson? Whatever became of him, the star for whom someone paid $100,000? Why, master Robertson is back with San Diego. Well, that's baseball."

His face flushed and he threw the paper on the floor—

It was someone knocking. All through the last paragraphs he had felt something interrupting his reading, but so intent had he been that he hadn't realized there was a knock on the door. Not a knock, either, a pounding now, as if someone were trying to break it down. His first thought was fire, but then he heard a familiar, if husky, voice the other side of the transom. He jumped up and threw it open as Razzle came in.

Tumbled in would better describe that entrance. Razzle's face was flushed and excited. The star's penchant for beer was famous, and stories were current of his experiences in former seasons, but so far this year he had been cautious. However, the long strain of pitching first-place ball, followed by the tight game of that afternoon, had been too much for him. Razzle was high.

His eye caught the open paper on the floor. The Kid flushed. But Razzle was not to be stopped. "Ha . . . ha! B'lieve what that mug says! Casey!" The scorn of years of baseball was in his voice. "Wha's he know about baseball . . . sittin' up there and tellin' us how to play the game. Like to see him handle a fogger a few times. . . ."

The Kid's attachment for Casey vanished. It was true. What did Casey know about it, or anyone who hadn't suffered out there on that mound inning after inning with the sun pitilessly beating upon your neck and the thermometer in the dugout at 120 degrees? No, Casey really didn't know. But the big fellow wanted action. He grabbed the paper and tearing it into pieces threw them outdoors. Then taking a huge chair he stumbled and lumbered across the room and, under the Kid's terrified eyes, shoved it through the window.

BANG! CRASH! BANG-BANG. The sound of breaking glass and splintering wood came from below, followed by shouts. The Kid jumped up and threw his arms round the big pitcher's body, only to find himself suddenly sprawling in a corner. Throwing him off like a fly, Razzle locked the door and began hauling another chair across the room.

Now there was a frenzied knocking, while from below came shouts and CRASH! BANG-BANG! CRASH! as a second chair went to destruction. The Kid made a dive for the door, but Razzle was too quick for him.

"No, you don't . . . either . . . I'm gonna give you the bum's rush too. . . ." And seizing the Kid by the shoulders he struggled toward the window. Surely the man wasn't insane enough . . .

"Hey, Razzle, Razzle, for Heaven's sake, leggo. . . . Hey, Razzle . . ."

Pound-pound, pound-pound from the door, and the exasperated voice of Gabby.

"Say there, open up that door, Tucker. I'll fine you plenty if you don't open up. . . ."

But the Kid couldn't open the door. Entwined in the arms of that ferocious bear he was unable to move. Vainly he struggled, yelled, shouted, caught the bottom of the bureau with his feet and managed to pull it over, yet still Razzle held him in a vise, still they neared the window. Then there was a crash. The door burst open. Five husky men jumped together on the luckless pitcher just before he had yanked the Kid to the sill of the tenth-story window.

His shirt completely ripped off, one shoe gone, his trousers torn in three pieces, a cut on his legs where he had hit something, disheveled, panting, exhausted, he stood watching them subdue the mighty Razzle. No easy matter either, for Razzle was in the mood for a roughhouse and gave as good as he got. Then two more men, apparently hotel detectives, joined them, and the combined forces managed, by pulling and hauling, to batter Razzle into submission, yank him into the shower, and gradually cool his ardor. It was two hours before the cuts, bleeding noses, and other evidences of battle were repaired, and things were back again at normal. The room being irretrievably wrecked, the Kid was changed, and Gabby, with Bill Hanson, the business manager, and Doc Masters, the trainer, attempted to conceal the conflict.

Unfortunately the news spread about the hotel as news of this kind will and, notwithstanding everything Gabby could do, the event was too sensational to cover up. The next morning Razzle's photograph was on all the front pages accompanied by a lurid account of the evening's foray, and a brief history of other and similar episodes

"LEMME GO, RAZZLE, LEMME GO——"

in former years. Within two hours Gabby had received a terse wire ordering him to submit a complete report immediately to the president of the League.

Result—for the team, one more man out of action. For Razzle, a month's suspension and a fine of $500. Expensive for a few glasses of beer.

12

The team was boarding the Manhattan Limited for New York. By the time of their departure from Pittsburgh more than half the squad presented some sort of problem, and the question was how a line-up could be made from the available players for the next afternoon at home. The club was feeling the strain of the race for the pennant. Reliable Tom Swanson was limping badly from an ankle which needed rest and time to heal; Jerry Strong was out for three weeks at least; Babe Stansworth, the big catcher, had a split thumb and was useless in games; Tommy Scudder had a fractured leg, the result of sliding home that day, and was left behind in a hospital; Fat Stuff, the steady old horse who did the relief pitching, was visiting Johns Hopkins for a lame arm; Karl Case in right was in a batting slump because the other men weren't hitting and he was asked to carry an unequal share of the load, while Gabby himself, beneath his tan, was drawn and tired about the eyes and wretchedly thin. His hitting had cooled off and his fielding lost its edge. Gabby needed a letup.

So did everyone else. Worst of all, Razzle, who merely had to take the box to have opposing hitters tighten up, was out for a month. A month during the most critical part of the season when the western clubs and the Giants were fighting desperately to grab away the slight lead the Dodgers held.

Going to the station in a taxi, the Kid's mind for some strange reason went back to the distance he had covered since Clearwater, and he began to reflect upon those hot weeks, a heat which now seemed as nothing. He recalled a remark of Rats Doyle, made after one of the first few days' practice as they came into the clubhouse together exhausted. It was one of the first times anyone had spoken to him or noticed him except old Dave Leonard, and he never forgot the remark or Doyle. "Spring training's the toughest part of it." The Kid smiled grimly at that sentence over a distance of six months. Somehow, looking back, spring training didn't seem so tough after all.

Bill Hanson, the business manager, stood at the train gate checking them in. Once this had seemed amazing to him; now it was simply routine.

"Stansworth . . . Case . . . Swanny . . . Tucker . . . Allen . . . Razzle . . . Foster . . . where's Fat Stuff? . . . Oh, yeah; he's down in Baltimore, isn't he? . . . Draper . . . Kennedy. . . ." As the Kid passed through the gate someone waiting stepped forward. It was Rex King of the New York *Times* who always accompanied the team on its western trip. He came up.

"Say, Tucker, would you mind coming through

to our compartment in the next car. Boys want a little information. . . ."

His first impulse was to say no. Why should he bother? One did; you had to; but why? What difference did it make? He didn't want them to write about him. Besides, he was tired and anxious to sleep. Some players could sleep until noon, but the Kid never. He was too used to getting up on the farm at home, doing the chores and putting in half a day's work before going to town to his job at MacKenzie's drugstore. He determined to refuse and was surprised to hear his voice say, "Sure, I'll go back with you." Mechanically he dropped his bag and his raincoat on his seat, took off his jacket, and went along with the older man to find four other newspapermen in the next car. They were sitting in a smoke-filled compartment, and hastily put away the cards on the table before them and drew out envelopes or pieces of folded paper. He knew what was ahead: an interview.

"Looks as if you men were going to make me talk after all." During the early part of the season he had managed to dodge interviews fairly successfully. Interviews were frightening, and the persistent questioning he received from sportswriters in the dugout before the game or in the locker room afterward in every city did little to reassure him.

"Say, you fellas, ever since I went to Clearwater back in March I been reading some interesting things about myself. But I didn't believe it was worth while to set things right. Too much trouble. Now it seems as if we might get the record straight."

The five men chorused assent. They were all certain that the other man had made the mistakes.

"Yep, that's what we want...."

"Okay, Kid, shoot the works now."

"Sure, le's go. Who discovered you? First of all, who discovered you? MacManus or..."

"Or Gabby...."

"Dave Leonard, wasn't it?" asked somebody.

"No, it wasn't." The Kid was positive because he was a trifle tired of that story. "It wasn't Dave and it wasn't Gabby and it wasn't really Mac, either. He came up to Waterbury last summer when I pitched one day, and old Hooks Barr, the owner, tried to get him to give me a chance. He wasn't interested. Much. Then at some league meeting or other, Hooks talked about me again, and kept at him until finally in the middle of winter he sent me money to come down and try out with the team. That's all."

"What about your borrowing the cash from your grandma to go down to Clearwater?"

He scowled. "Aw, that's the bunk. They sent me the dough all right, but we had to use it to replace the roof which got damaged in that storm last fall. Come winter, it started to leak so badly in the kitchen we had to use the money for that. So I did and borrowed some cash from my grandma. See?" The five men were scribbling furiously. He wondered what there was in his remarks to enable them to fill up all that space.

"Is it true you sat up all night in the day coach?..."

The Kid was tired. Hot and tired and bored.

"What's that got to do with it anyhow?" The pencils went to work round the table again.

"Tell us about your life. Where were you born?"

"Tomkinsville."

"Live at home?"

"Yep . . . I live with my grandma on the farm. Dad died when I was a kid and my mother died two years ago."

"Work on the farm?"

"Uhuh. But I work in town too. At MacKenzie's drugstore."

"You work at home and in town . . ."

"Why, sure. I don't go on the day shift until noon. Noon to eight at night." What time did they think folks got up on a farm?

They changed the subject. "What great pitcher did you model yourself after?"

"No great pitcher." There was a silence in the compartment. He didn't model himself after anyone. Why should he? "My only thought was to get on the Dodgers and stick there . . . if I could." He paused a moment. "Y'see, I'm not a very good story. I'm not a mystery story. I don't count myself a great pitcher. Had lots of luck, and a lot of help from old Dave Leonard. Maybe he ought to get the credit." He noticed several raised eyebrows, and glances exchanged across the table. The four men were scribbling furiously. "First place my curve ball is too slow. Dave was working to give me a faster hook. I never fan many, and I . . . I never forget I've got a swell ballclub out there working their heads off for me all the time. There . . . is that enough? . . . I'm tired, you guys. . . ."

It was enough. Until the next time. The next time came sooner than any of them expected. In fact within twenty-four hours.

There was one thing the Kid never got accustomed to, and that was the difference in the dressing room after a game they lost and a game they won. If they lost, the fatigue of the afternoon seemed doubled; everyone was all in and showed it, nerves were edgy, dressing was hard work, although nobody wanted to stay in the tension of the room any longer than necessary.

But when they won! And when they won over the Giants! MacManus and Murphy were exchanging barbed pleasantries in the newspapers, but the closeness of the league standing was enough to pack the stands that afternoon without additional help. Both teams were keen to win. The Dodgers wanted to stretch their lead to three full games, the Giants to cut it down to one game, and incidentally grab off second place. But they were helpless before the Kid. Never had he felt keener, never more like pitching, and even with their patched line-up three runs were enough. That brought his victorious record up to fifteen. The fans almost mobbed him as he came off the field, and directly he reached the safety of the dressing room, the reporters were on his neck again.

The place was hot, dusty, and noisy, jubilant because everyone was singing and shouting across the room. A three-game lead, with a substitute catcher, a second string at third, and a utility outfielder playing most of the game, wasn't bad. The room echoed and re-echoed to their yells, and the boys slapped him on the back as they came in throwing their gloves at their lockers.

"Nice work, Roy, old kid. . . ."

"Tha's pitching, that is, Roy. . . ."

"Boy, were you hot today. . . ."

"Great stuff, Kid; that's keeping ahead of those batters all right, all right. . . ."

MacManus came across the room to his locker. "Roy, that's pitching, and it's about time we did something for you. Drop into the office tomorrow — No, tomorrow I'm in Boston. Drop in Thursday or Friday. I've torn up your old contract and we've got to make out a new one."

A new contract! His old one called for a couple of thousand dollars, which had seemed a fortune when he signed it early in April. A new contract. That meant more. Real money. Now he would be fixed, for Jack MacManus was a real guy.

Soon the sportswriters, having finished their stories, came in. They drifted nonchalantly across the room pretending not to see him, laughing and kidding, but with their eye fixed upon their prey. They surrounded his bench and stood watching him like an animal in the zoo, as he peeled off his sweaty undershirt, his pants, his soggy stockings. Question after question was thrown at him. How did he feel? . . . Was he nervous out there? . . . Did the record help his pitching? . . . Would he? . . . Did he? . . . Could he? . . .

"Wait a minute, you guys. Lemme have a shower, will yuh?"

"Yeah, sure, let him have his shower," they replied in unison as he went across to the steaming water.

There were laughter and shouts coming from the shower, boisterous cries and yells. Immediately upon stepping into the warm water he was soothed, refreshed and relaxed. His muscles stopped aching. The tired feeling in his body slowly disappeared, and a great contentment took possession of his frame. Outside, the boys were horsing round, slapping each other with the ends of wet towels . . . calling names, someone suggesting a movie to someone else . . . when it happened.

Like that. Suddenly. One minute he was up, then he was on the floor, before he could save himself or do anything. Tom Swanson, standing just outside the shower, jumped quickly to avoid a wet towel-end, and as he did so fell against the Kid in the beating curtain of water. Blinded, the Kid stepped further in . . . slipped . . . and fell. On his elbow. His right elbow. There was a stinging pain.

Someone reached in and hauled him up and out. Dripping wet, in a hush, and a deep silence. Doc Masters at the far end of the room curtly left someone on the rubbing table and ran to where the Kid was sitting on a bench, his face twisted in pain, feeling of his injured elbow. From nowhere a circle gathered, men with towels in their hands, men half-dressed, naked, reporters, players, all with serious faces. Then Gabby with only his pants on came pushing and shoving through the circle, cursing.

"How many times have I told you men . . . Who did that? . . . Who shoved you, Tuck? . . . How many times I've said . . . Is it okay, Doc, is it okay, is it? . . ."

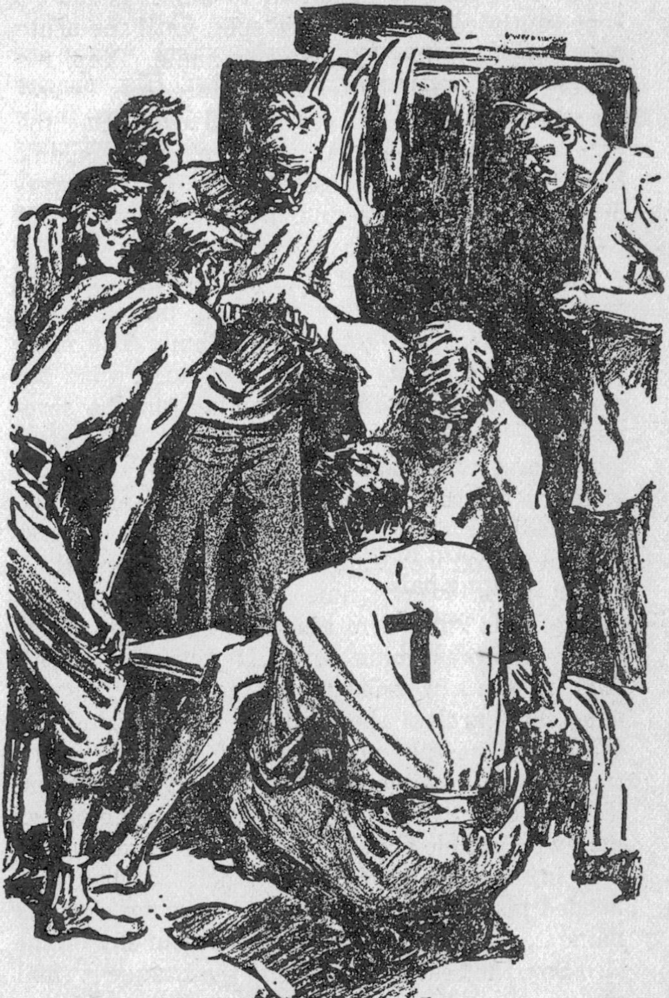

"IS IT OKAY, DOC? IS IT OKAY?"

The Doc paid no attention to him. Instead he kept gently rubbing the sore spot, until the acute pain subsided. The Kid tried to smile. "Yep, it's better now, much better." His face was sweating; in fact he was sweating all over. But the pain was less violent. A few days' rest wouldn't hurt him anyhow, Doc suggested. He was overdrawn. He was down fine. But the elbow would be okay; nothing serious about that.

The reporters weren't sure. They didn't want to miss a story if there was one, but yet they weren't anxious to get out on a limb. The news spread. Once in his room in the hotel with his arm bandaged and liniment taking out the soreness, the telephone rang. Newspapers, radio commentators, press associations, everyone wanted to know whether he had been injured and if so how badly. Finally in despair he told the operator not to connect him, and slowly undressed. A dozen times, twenty times, a hundred times, he fingered his right arm tenderly, trying to decide if the pain was going down. It was a hot night. And he was a worried boy as he lay thinking of what one careless shove might do, realizing for the first time the importance of physical condition and its possible effect on his paycheck. Stories he'd heard came back; locker room gossip of men who got blood poisoning, who received leg or arm injuries which cut short their baseball life, flooded his brain. That catcher . . . what was his name . . . on the Browns . . . And Donnelly of the Red Sox, the best left-hander in the League . . . and the young rookie from the Coast who lost his leg from an infected spike wound . . . yes, and Fat

Stuff, who was trying to nurse a weak arm along....

As he turned over he realized suddenly that it wasn't called his salary arm for nothing.

13

Whenever Grandma was in trouble she made tea. Whenever she was tired and exhausted and worried from trying to keep the farm going with the help of the young Johnson boy next door and a hired man seldom reliable, she brewed tea. Strong tea. Tea occupied much the same place in her life that beer did in Razzle Nugent's. Inasmuch as she was not in training she availed herself of her particular stimulant more often.

Grandma knew baseball. Being the grandmother of the Kid, she had to. But she had learned much from his letters and from the New York newspapers to which he subscribed for her. She not only understood the game, but also the casual significances which lay behind newspaper stories or the patter of the radio announcer. When Roy was pitching she always had the radio tuned in, a new magnificent machine with short wave and other facilities that Grandma scorned.

"Now that was bad of him, real bad of him, buying that expensive thing. I wish he'd save his money. Besides I'd just as lief have kept the old one; fact is I was kinder fond of it." So she was, but the Kid knew she'd never get Cincinnati and St. Louis on the older set.

The radio was chattering while she rose and left the room to make tea. Despite the view over the back meadows where the hired man was mowing steadily, the kitchen seemed cheerless. She bent over and with a vigorous gesture turned down the arrows of the kerosene stove. Roy had wanted her to have a gas range, but she put her foot down. Gas was dangerous. Always she had cooked by coal in winter and kerosene in summer, and always she would. Moving to the sink she pumped water into a tea kettle and placed it on the stove, struck a match and lighted the soaking wicks of the kerosene stove.

"Click-click-click-click-click-click," came the familiar sound of the machine in the meadow, and the hired man's peculiar way of addressing the horses.

"Oopse, there, Sandy, oopse. . . ."

Grandma stood listening, her gaze on the back road and the distant hills, hills she had seen as a child and as a woman, a sight so accustomed that from the window over the sink she actually saw nothing. What she saw was a wide green field dotted with men in white and a boy standing alone in the middle, his hands on his hips. He was in trouble. What the trouble was she couldn't tell, yet something was wrong. A voice from the other room called her back again to the kitchen in the farm.

She returned to the parlor and sat down in the rocker before the radio. "Now, folks, that makes three men on base, three on and nobody out. First three Boston batters have singled, Kline's hit was a clean smack to left and only fast fielding prevented a run. Roy Tucker out there on the mound . . . looks unhappy. . . . He's rubbing his right arm. . . . Now Gabby's coming in from short to talk to him. . . . Remember, this will be his sixteenth straight win, folks,

no rookie ever won sixteen straight his first year before, and no pitcher in the League, in either league, ever won more. . . ."

"There they go. He's set . . . his foot goes up

. . . first pitch . . . is . . . wide, ball one. Ball one. *Is* this crowd nuts! They sure want to see the Dodgers get back into first place by taking this game, and they're all out there pulling for that Kid in the box. Here comes the pitch, ball two. Isn't a very good start. What's the matter, Roy? He doesn't seem ahead of the hitters the way he usually is. Two balls, two and none . . . there it goes, a hit . . . a fly to deep center. . . . Swanny's going back . . . back . . . he's up against the fence now . . . IT'S . . . A HOME RUN. . . ." And his voice was lost in a tremendous roar.

"Well, I guess that was a little lucky. Pretty lucky, that was, just cleared the fence, a few feet this way it'd 'a' been out. Kelley went for the cripple and knocked it over the fence, and that means four runs. Four runs isn't so much against this scrappy ballclub . . . now the boys are round the box talking to him, and Gabby's slapping him on the back; they're still behind him. Here comes Chick Duffy, the Braves' right fielder, bats .285. . . ."

"Strike one. . . ." Again that terrific roar filled Grandma's sitting room. "There's the old Tucker, burning his fast one in there for a called strike. Here's the pitch, wide . . . a ball . . . one and one . . . nobody down, first inning in this game between the Dodgers and the Braves here at Ebbets Field. . . . Here it comes . . . he hits . . . down the left foul line . . . Scudder's after it . . . Duffy rounding first . . . he takes second safely . . . Duffy cracks a double to left, that's the fourth straight hit against Tucker. . . . Just hear that crowd yell."

Grandma wiped her face nervously. Outside

from the meadow the sounds of the mower persisted, "click-click, click-click, click-click," as though nothing mattered but the cutting of the hay.

"Rubino, Boston catcher . . . bats .305 . . . a dangerous man. Duffy dancing off second . . . the Kid watches over his shoulder . . . his leg goes up . . . here it comes . . . Tony hits . . . a clean single to center . . . Duffy on third, coming home . . . Swanson throws to the plate . . . but Gabby cuts it off to prevent Rubino taking second on the throw-in. Say . . . the fifth straight hit, fifth run scored . . ."

Now the yelling drowned his voice. It lasted for what seemed eternity to Grandma. She understood perfectly what had happened. Roy was tired. He should have had a good rest, a week at home with good cooking, not the hotel stuff he had to eat. Imagine. A boy like him trying to pitch baseball games twice a week through a hot summer. It was outrageous.

". . . and . . . yes . . . yes . . . there he goes . . . yep, Gabby is beckoning old Fat Stuff Foster from the bullpen, and Fat Stuff is pretending not to see him and throwing a couple of fast ones, 'cause he was caught a little short there, no one expected the Kid to be yanked like this. Guess the boy is overworked . . ." here Grandma raised her head quickly in approval . . . "he's going to the showers now and the crowd is giving him a great hand, hear 'em . . ." The roar was enormous, it kept rising louder and louder and she could hardly hear the voice of the announcer. ". . . seems to be rubbing his elbow . . . crowd still cheering . . . they're all disappointed he came so close to the record without making it . . . Draper and Cassidy, the coaches, are running up, Draper has his arm round him, asking him something . . . now Fat Stuff is coming into the box, Fat Stuff Foster, No. 6, taking the place of Roy Tucker, No. 56, in the box for Brooklyn, the score four to nothing . . . correction . . . five to nothing for Boston in the first inning, no one out and a man on first. . . ."

Grandma leaned over and snapped off the radio. She knew, or felt she knew, what had happened. Too much. He'd been given too much work. There was silence in the room, yet still through the kitchen window came the eternal click-click, click-click, click-click of the mower in the meadow below the house. Then another noise, a kind of hissing sound from the kitchen. The water was boiling. Grandma jumped up. In her lean body and the way she yanked the kettle from the stove were the same lines and the same gesture of a boy who walked across a sunswept diamond and threw his glove with a jerk into the dugout.

14

Dozens of children stood or sat on wooden benches with their parents waiting for their turn to be called. It was hardly a cheerful spot. Most of them were on crutches, had splints on legs or arms, or worse still, wore iron braces. He passed quickly through the big room used as a clinic. In the corridors cool nurses looked at him curiously, and orderlies walking by glanced at his tanned face; a face now familiar to readers of the sports pages. And to everyone connected with the hospital because they all knew about the Kid from Tomkinsville and his injury.

Down the corridor round a corner he came to a room which had the words "X RAY" on the door. Stripping to the waist, he was placed on a cold table while a murderous-looking machine suspended on an iron arm was poised above his shoulder. It pointed like a huge gun at his heart. Two silent nurses hovered about, twisting and turning the gun, and from time to time an intern popped in to watch proceedings.

"Now, then," she said briskly. "Please hold your breath . . . ready. . . ." A light flashed somewhere, and the machine whirred and buzzed. They photoed him on his back and on his face. They snapped him from every angle, high and low; they took pictures from both sides. The Kid lay there, patiently obeying orders, wondering when they would ever have enough but willing to go on as long as necessary if only he could get his arm back in shape.

Funny thing, it felt all right, even when he pitched. He could throw his curve as well as ever, but the moment he tried to bear down, the second he attempted to shoot his fast one in, there was a stinging pain above the elbow which slowed up his delivery. Moreover, the longer he pitched, the worse the pain became. A week's rest did no good, and even after ten days his arm was in the same condition when he went out to pitch to the batters.

Meanwhile his injury hurt the club. With the Kid useless, with Razzle still out, the other pitchers were overworked and soon felt the effect of too much pitching. Gabby, who was a hard loser, began to get plenty of practice. From first place the team slipped down to second and then third. The strain was telling all round. Roommates suddenly burst into anger because the man with them used their toothbrush by mistake. Fights broke out; gradually the team morale, which had been buoyed and sustained by the tenseness of their drive for the pennant, cracked. Gabby stormed and raged against the other teams, he harried the umpires more incessantly than ever, he prodded and pricked the men on the squad continually. All to no good purpose. They kept dropping.

"Y'see, it's like this, Mac." He was sitting with his feet against MacManus' large mahogany desk one morning toward the end of August. "There's one thing a first-division club must have, and that's a pitcher who can go in there and stop a losing streak. If the team is going badly and has lost three or four games in a row, and you have a guy like Sweeney of the Red Sox or Buck Temple of the Yanks, or Razzle, for instance, who can jump in and stop it—well, you aren't going to be hurt much. It's that losing streak we fell into after Tucker got hurt that did the damage."

"Right. I sure wish we could get Tucker back. Now an operation . . ."

Gabby snorted. "Operations! Once those babies get hold of you all bets are off. When the surgeons start putting a knife to a pitcher's arm you can count on its taking him a year to come round at the very least. If he does then. Look at Jack Sampson, look at Spike Hallahan, look at . . . Why, there's dozens I've seen. Myself, I think it's a chipped bone, that's all; it interferes with the locking of the joint like this, see. . . ." He flexed his arm. "Lots of pitchers have chipped bones that heal up and don't hurt 'em. Tony Krause of the Reds had one last year and all he did was win seventeen games."

"Hope you're right. A chipped bone inside the hinge mechanism means an operation, but I believe they can straighten it out. He'll be okay next year. I'm only afraid it isn't that. Anyhow we'll soon know. I was supposed to call the Doc this morning." He took off the receiver. "Miss Swan, get me Doctor Jackson at the Ruptured and Crippled Hospital.

"Yeah, Doctor Jackson . . . MacManus speaking . . . oh, good morning, Doctor. Yessir, yessir, pretty good, how're you? That's fine. Have you seen those X rays of young Tucker yet? You have. . . . How's it look to you?" He fiddled with his eyeglasses on the table as he talked. Gabby listened, watching his face. "Yep . . . I see. . . ." A slight frown came over his freckled countenance. The natural cheery look faded. "I see. Oh, you don't. . . . You don't think so. . . ." The frown deepened. "An operation won't . . . won't do the trick, hey?" Now the frown became a scowl. "Well, yes, I should think so." There was perspiration on his forehead and he passed the back of his hand quickly across it. "All right, I'll come down and talk things over." He reached for his desk calendar. "Say tomorrow at three . . . at two-thirty then. Fine. Thanks." He rang off with a gesture.

For just a moment he looked out the window, hating to see that anxious, nervous face before him.

"Gabby, I know you can take it all right; only hope the Kid can. I'm afraid you mustn't count on him, you'll have to carry on . . . he'll never pitch again."

There was a moment's silence. But Gabby was a fighter. "Whaddya mean he'll never pitch again! Mac, you don't mean to take it from those medicos, do you? Why, they always make mistakes. I remember when I was on the Cards we had two men . . ."

"No, I don't. We'll check on this. He'll go down to Johns Hopkins tomorrow. But this man knows his stuff. Just what I was afraid; it isn't as easy as a chipped bone. An operation might cure that. But it's what he calls epicondylitis. Well, that's his term. Means there's a sort of calcification of the muscles. I have a letter here about it all. He says it's caused by . . . 'a pulling of the external epicondyle,' whatever that is. They took over fifty pictures from special oblique rays which show the whole darn thing. He thinks the Kid won't ever be any good again in the box. The Doc is a fan too."

Gabby was unconvinced. He knew doctors and still hoped. The Kid hoped also. Cracking like that in one game meant nothing, especially after such a long winning streak. Why, all freshman pitchers felt the effects of trying to keep up their victories; look at Rice of the Yanks and Rogerson of the Cards. When they finally lost, the result was a slump, always. Naturally. That crack on the elbow, he was sure, had nothing at all to do with it. This was the way he reasoned in Johns Hopkins where he stayed over a week and got what he needed most of all, a rest, a change from the grind of baseball.

In between X rays and consultations they worked on the Kid's arm twice a day. First they baked it for thirty minutes under a powerful lamp, and then a Swedish masseur spent an hour on it, gently and soothingly at first, more vigorously every time. The little man knew his business. Within two days the Kid noticed a difference. The rest, or the baking, or the treatment, or all three together, made him feel able to jump in and pitch a nineteen-inning game. So he told the doctor-in-chief, for he wanted to return to the boys. But the man in the long white coat shook his head.

"Not just yet. We haven't quite finished examinations yet. We need a few more pictures of the arm, and then I'd like to have you take a couple more treatments . . . if you feel they do you good."

"They sure do. The old whip feels just fine, Doc. As loose as ashes."

The older man shook his head queerly and said nothing. Instead he took the arm in his hands, holding it by the wrist and the elbow, moving it slowly round in a circle, bending it forward, pulling it out straight. Then he held it carefully and looked closely at it, and after that went through the same motions, bending, turning, straightening. Always the same questions.

"That hurt . . . that . . . or that . . . any pain . . . ?"

No, there was no pain, no soreness, no stiffness whatever. The Kid wondered why the doctor stood looking at the arm with such a puzzled expression.

It was ten days before they let him go and he was able to rejoin the team in Chicago. Around the lobby of the Congress that morning were half a dozen of the boys who descended upon him with delight, glad to have him back because the Dodgers were now in third and only a game and a half from fourth. Gabby came across the lobby with quick, nervous steps, eager for news, beaming when reassured that the arm had healed.

"Why, sure. It was just a whack on the bone,

needs rest, that's all. I've seen lots of 'em. Pitchers take worse than that and come back; I told Mac so at home last week. Look at Grove, look at Hubbell, look at Rowe. . . . Why, they're all pitching good ball, ain't they? Of course. . . ."

When they took the field a few days later, the Kid grinned at Gabby's admonition to take it easy. Never had he felt more anxious to pitch, and it was not easy to watch Jake and Fat Stuff and Rats, all overworked and fine, go out to the mound when he was in such trim. Maybe he'd get in a few innings as a relief pitcher if one was needed. If not, they'd surely pitch him in turn tomorrow or the next day.

"Easy, now, Kid," warned Gabby again.

He grinned back. It was wonderful to be with them all again, to hear Gabby's familiar bark: "All right, gang; le's go" . . . to feel the sun on the back of his neck, to stand in the bullpen between Jake and Fat Stuff. A small knot of spectators collected close by to watch him pitch. Well, they'd see something.

The arm was never better. He started carefully by warming up gently, tossing in a few idle balls. Then came ten or fifteen minutes of slow balls, after which he shoved his glove under his left armpit and massaged his other arm the way they did in the hospital. The afternoon was hot and he felt no soreness or stiffness of any kind, so after several more medium pitches he let his wrist go limp and snapped in his fast one. It took a beautiful hop, that hop which made his old fast ball so effective. The old stuff was there.

Around and from both sides his watching teammates exclaimed.

"That's the old stuff, Roy. . . ."

"That's burning it in, Kid."

"Right in the slot, Roy. Any pain?"

Gabby's approval had a questioning tone. Pain? No, not a trace. Not a bit of feeling anywhere. He threw over a couple more medium pitches and then his curve. But something happened. The ball refused to break. He tried it quickly again with the same result. His slider was all right. The hop was there on his fast one. But his curve . . .

Suddenly he became panicky and, wiping his forehead with the back of his hand, he noticed he was sweating violently. That curve now, funny thing about his curve. He wound up slowly and put everything he had on the ball. No good, it just wasn't there.

Then the pain came. For the first time he felt a twinge, a distinct catch as he tried to throw the curve. The twinge deepened the more he pitched until even Gabby noticed it. In five minutes the twinge had become a sullen, growing pain. Still he couldn't get any snap to the number 2.

No use. He was finished. Tossing his glove to the ground he walked to the dugout. Gabby clapped him on the back and said something about more rest, but as the Kid slumped in despair on the bench he knew. His curve was gone. He was through. Without a curve he was half a pitcher, or rather no pitcher at all. By this time the rest of the boys knew it too. The fielders paused for a moment by the bullpen to speak to the other pitchers. He could tell by their sudden warm concern when they came back to the water cooler for a drink, or stopped to grab a bat from the rack just in front of his seat. There was something in the way they looked into his eyes, wondering how he'd take it, which convinced him.

It was possible, it was likely, he'd never pitch again.

Never pitch again! Never have that feeling of sweet fatigue at the end of a tough victory, no, never sniff again the smell of the locker room, that peculiar smell of sweat-ridden garments and men's perspiring bodies mixed with the ointments and unguents from the rubbing table, never see the familiar black tin trunks with the red bands and the big letters in red on the top: BROOKLYN BASEBALL CLUB. Never see the boys: Gabby and Fat Stuff and Razzle and Red Allen and the others. Why, say, these men were his friends. In the papers they were just names in the line-up: Davis 2b, Scudder lf, Swanson cf, Strong 3b, Nugent pitcher. But to him they were individuals: Jerry who always insisted on carrying his own heavy bag, Razzle who never ate breakfast, Rats Doyle who wouldn't ride in a taxi before he pitched. They were comrades by what they had gone through, and more, they were men who'd saved him in tight places, who had suddenly come up with a doubleplay ball from nowhere, who had crashed into the fences of St. Louis and Pittsburgh and Chicago to pull him out of bad holes, who had risked spiking or worse to get a man when every out counted double at critical moments. Now he was leaving them. Leaving these men, his friends.

It couldn't be true. Something would be done, surely something could be done, some sort of an operation. Mac had promised, Mac had told him he would spend as much money as necessary to get the best medical attention. He'd have it out with Gabby that evening and learn how things were and where they stood. Gabby would know. But Gabby for some reason didn't show up for dinner, and later someone remarked they'd seen him drive off alone in his big blue cabriolet, a habit of his when he was worried and things weren't breaking right. He liked to think out his problems alone on the road. No, Gabby wasn't in a good mood, but he'd have to be tackled even though the Dodgers had just lost their fourth straight game and were in fifth place that evening. Gabby, too, had plenty to worry over.

Desolate and lonely, the Kid wandered into a movie. The picture meant nothing; he couldn't watch it and, leaving the theater, he returned to the hotel at nine-thirty. Razzle was standing in the doorway conversing with Swanny, and he paused as they asked for news of his condition. The pitchers, like everyone else, were anxious to see him back on the mound.

"How're you feeling, Kid?" said Razzle. He tried to be cheerful.

"Oh, I'm feeling kinder non-careless, as Pepper Martin would say."

Razzle started to speak. Then there was a roar, a screeching of brakes, and a taxi stopped. The door opened and Casey, hatless, disheveled, redder of face than ever, jumped out. He nearly knocked them over rushing into the lobby as rapidly as his chunky body permitted.

Razzle looked at Swanny and Swanny looked at the Kid. "What's biting Casey?" The taxi stood like a sweating horse, puffing at the curb.

"LENOX HILL HOSPITAL—

AS FAST AS YOU CAN!"

"Aw, he's nuts, that bum. Said I was in a batting slump, and the afternoon they ran the piece I smacked out a double and two singles," interjected the center fielder, neglecting to mention that he had then gone hitless for three games in a row.

"Tell yuh what's the trouble with them sportswriters, they all think . . ."

Razzle stopped. He stopped because he saw the other two were not listening. They were watching the excited face of Casey burst through the door, jump with a leap into the taxi, and shout to the driver:

"Lenox Hill. Lenox Hill Hospital, fast as you can!"

To the Kid the astonishing thing about the sportswriters was their ability always to pop up from nowhere when something happened. Late at night, long after the club was abed, early in the morning before they had risen, in St. Louis or Cincinnati, among the sand dunes of Florida, in hotels or trains, in busses or locker rooms, no matter where the club was, they were always on the job when something happened. How they found out trouble was afoot he never knew. But they always did. He was not, therefore, surprised to see Rex King of the *Times* jump from another taxi, followed shortly after by Sandy Martin of the *Post* who appeared from the subway exit.

"What's up? The boys look kinda worried." Neither man stopped to speak as usual, but ran into the hotel. While the three players stood speculating, Fat Stuff Foster sauntered out from the lobby.

"Hey, what's eating Casey? He nearly

knocked me down a piece back there trying to make the door."

They didn't know. No one knew, and they were about to go in and question them when the two reporters reappeared, talking rapidly.

"I tell you a taxi's quicker."

"Nope, Rex, the subway . . ."

"Yeah, if you nab an express. But then you hafta change at Grand Central for a local. Here, hey there, taxi! C'mon, Sandy, come with me."

"Look here, you guys!" Fat Stuff stepped to the curb as they hopped into the taxi without a word to the players beside the door. "What's up?"

Martin stuck his face out the window while the taxi moved down the street.

"Gabby . . . Gabby," he shouted back. "In an auto accident on the Parkway. Won't last out the night."

15

The Kid was overjoyed to see him back with the club. So were all the other players.

The rest of baseball took little notice of Dave Leonard's appointment as manager of the Dodgers in place of Gabby. Because the Dodgers were going down, down. Brooklyn in first or second meant something. Brooklyn in sixth place was normal. Dave had a thankless task and a hopeless one. As Jim Casey put it in his column:

"Everyone likes Dave Leonard of the Dodgers, a grand guy, and everyone wishes him luck with the Flatbush Flounders. But a man would have to be a combination of John McGraw, Connie Mack, and all the great managers of the game to start the Daffy Dodgers upward. Let's wish him the best, turn our heads the other way quickly, and hope his sentence won't be long."

Murphy of the Giants was less polite when he heard the news. "Last spring I said Philadelphia was the only team the Dodgers could beat. Now it looks like I was optimistic."

For once MacManus did not retort. Gabby had been a friend of many years; he had known the peppy little shortstop in other cities and brought him as manager to Brooklyn. Naturally the sudden death of the leader rocked him badly. He would merely say,

"I've got confidence in Dave Leonard, which is why I've called him back, and he's going to have the full support of the management here, just as Gabby always had."

However regretted Gabby was, the umpires unanimously sighed with relief. Gabby invariably made their life miserable. On the team, too, there was a let-down in tension. The pitchers were looser in the box, the batters didn't tighten up, the team spirit was better. To the Kid, Gabby's accident was a shock, and he was amazed by the way things went along without him. In baseball no one was necessary.

Because the team won, the team lost, the team played and played well enough, without Gabby. Its suddenness too was typical of baseball. A rookie made a name for himself overnight, a man was on top, and then in a matter of hours he was out of the picture. There was something terrifying about the pace of the game, the way men moved in, up, and out. Had Dave Leonard returned a few weeks before, Roy would have been the happiest man in the League. Now with his career finishing and his departure imminent, the sight of the genial, quiet-voiced catcher back in their midst only made things worse.

Dave's first move was to shake up the batting order. He yanked Swanson, who was in a slump, and put in Gaines, a substitute. He pulled Eddie Davis and threw in a second string infielder named Whitehouse. He shook the batting order up completely, placing Gaines in the clean-up position and moving Strong to lead-off man. Two days after Gabby's death the Kid entered the lobby of the hotel to see a face he knew and couldn't place at first, a solemn face from which two big brown eyes looked out. Then the Kid recognized the face as well as the brown sports coat and the loud-checked trousers of its owner. Harry Street!

"Boy! Am I glad to see you. . . . Back with the team?"

"Why, Roy! Say . . . it's swell to see you again. How you feeling? I didn't know you'd be here. You sure look good. The old whip okay?"

The Kid's face fell. "Harry, come upstairs. We can talk up there." In his room he explained what had happened, how doctors in three cities had been examining and X raying his arm, how he had taken all sorts of treatment without relief. He would never pitch again.

"Gosh. That right?" The solemn face became even more serious. "Whatcha gonna do then? They can't let you out, can they . . . until fall?"

"No. They can't afford to keep me, either. I'm no doggone use like this to anyone."

But yet Dave kept him on the roster. A month before he was the star pitcher of the League, unable to enter a hotel dining room without half a dozen autograph fiends pestering him; now he was forgotten, Tucker, No. 56, a rookie. The fans had quick memories. Harry Street at shortstop was already making them forget Gabby Spencer, and the general opinion was that he filled the hole even better than could be expected. There seemed no place for the Kid, yet Dave still kept him on.

It was strange watching games every afternoon from the bench instead of the field. Day after day he sat in the dugout while his teammates struggled before his eyes. Once he actually got a paste at the ball. Rats Doyle had been hit hard in a close game and withdrawn, and when his turn to bat came in the last of the ninth against the Cubs, the Kid was sent in. His single won the game.

The next afternoon when he finished batting practice Dave stepped from behind the screen.

"Roy, Charlie Draper and I been watching you just now. I think I could show you how to improve your hitting. You got a good free swing there, but you'll never be a first-class hitter with that grip. Now take ahold of that bat. Yes, your regular way. . . . See what I mean?" And he pushed the Kid's hands several inches up the handle. "Now grip it like that. Choke it. A little more . . . there . . . that's about right. . . . Choke your bat. Now here, let me throw you a few. Oh, sure, I know what you'll say. . . ."

"Don't feel natural."

"Of course not . . . at first. But you'll get used to it and once you do you'll be a much better hitter. Now one more thing. You're hitting under the ball. Your stride's too long. Shorten up that stride as you hit the ball. Like this . . . see. Here's the way you stride . . . get me? Okay, go in there and see how it feels at the plate."

Well, Dave ought to know. Dave had seen hitters come and go, Dave could tell. But it felt awkward, and the shortened stride bothered him at first. After a while, however, he found it easier, and he began to like it a little. He took another turn at bat after Dave had thrown some more, correcting his stance all the time, and it went better.

But meanwhile as days went past, MacManus said nothing about the new contract. Things had changed since the fateful tumble in the shower, nor indeed did the Kid expect a new contract, for he realized he was now a liability and would be sent home any day. However, Dave took him along on their next western trip in September when the Dodgers were fighting for a berth in the first division. Four times the Kid was used as pinch hitter, once drawing a base on balls, striking out once, and hitting safely twice. The longer he used that new grip and the different stance the more he liked it, and every morning he used to go to the ball park for an hour's practice with one of the pitchers who would throw to him.

It helped to find he still had some slight value. The team came back to the Polo Grounds for a critical series with the Giants who needed every game in their fight for the pennant. As much as the Dodgers wanted every game to make the first division. Sportswriters said that Mac was giving Dave a chance to see what he could do. If the club made the first division he would be given a contract for the next season; if not, he would be released.

The Giants took the opener against Fat Stuff Foster, two to one, while the second was won by Jake Kennedy in a pitching duel, one to nothing. The third was a hitting game. Rats Doyle was knocked out early, so was Chuck Sweeney, the Giant star, and the score rose to seven to five as they went into the ninth. Harry Street, who had been leading the club in batting since his return, pasted the ball to left center for two bases. Jerry followed with a scratch single, and Staines, the New York relief pitcher, was yanked.

Men on first and third, no one out. Dave motionless on the bench, leading the team by the movements of his scorecard up and down or sideways, saying nothing, his cap over his eyes, a contrast to the active, noisy Gabby who rode miles along the bench every game and was never silent. Case, the next batter, stood at the plate. The ball was low and wide, and on a double steal play Harry on third made a dart for home. The Giant shortstop came in back of the pitcher, intercepted the throw and tossed it to the plate, but Harry had whirled back and was sliding into third, while Jerry was safe at second. A hit meant two runs. But Case popped to second and there were two out. Up to the plate lumbered big Babe Stansworth, the catcher. He was a good hitter. The Giants knew it too, and he drew a base on balls for Razzle Nugent, the pitcher, was the next man up.

Dave leaned over and called down the bench, "Roy, go in there and bring those boys home." The Kid's heart jumped. His hopes were justified; maybe Dave was keeping him for use as a pinch hitter. Stepping from the dugout, he picked up two bats and walked confidently to the plate.

"Tucker . . . No. 56 . . . batting for Nugent . . . No. 37 . . . for Brooklyn. . . ." A ripple of applause ran through the stands. Memories were short, but apparently they hadn't all forgotten the pitcher who lost his arm in mid-season. From the box he could hear a murmur in the crowd as he tossed away one bat and stepped forward. Here was his chance. His big chance at last.

The runners hopped about the basepaths with open arms. Already the diamond was in shadow, and the cool chill of a fall evening was in the air. From the coaching lines came the familiar voices of Charlie Draper and old Cassidy. Here was his chance. He braced himself for the pitch, swung . . .

And missed.

It was a curve and he was well over the ball. His old fault. The stands yelled approval. To be beaten was one thing, to be beaten by the sixth-place Dodgers in a critical moment was something else.

"Take a cut at it, Roy. . . ." Draper's voice came through the clear evening air. From the other side he heard Cassidy's familiar "Knock his turkey neck offen him, Kid. C'mon now, le's go, le's go. . . ." He tried hard to remember what he had been told, to shorten his stride. The ball came and he gave it everything he had, but he was late.

It fouled off back to the screen. "Strike two . . ." shouted Stubblebeard, the umpire, with what sounded like triumph in his voice.

Two and none. The Kid became cautious and watched the next one wide of the corner.

"Make him come in there, Roy. Give it a belt now." There it was, a good . . . a clean . . . he leaned forward and swung with all his might, only to hear the sound he had so often longed to hear from the box, the sound of the ball plunking into the catcher's mitt. Tossing the ball in the air and tucking his mask under his arm, the man behind the plate turned and raced for the showers. Three strikes. The game was over.

Dressing in the atmosphere of that locker room was not pleasant. He got away as soon as he could, took the subway back to Brooklyn and went to a little restaurant where he would find none of the team. Not that he wanted anything to eat; it was just something to do, to take his mind off himself, off his dismal failure. His chance, his one big chance, and he'd muffed it. In a week he'd be home now, trying to get a job on the night shift at MacKenzie's drugstore.

Then he heard his name. At the next table two men were talking.

"How'd the Dodgers come out?"

"Oh . . . they lost as usual. That big stiff Tucker struck out with three on in the ninth. Whoever told that ham he could hit? Leonard must be nuts if he thinks that kind of ball will . . ."

The Kid pulled a dollar from his pocket, slipped it under his plate and walked quickly out the door. He had heard enough. Down the street was a coffee shop where he might be left in peace. But halfway through his meat and potatoes, someone behind him started the same refrain. He heard a newspaper rustle. Then a voice.

"See where the Dodgers took it on the chin again today?"

"Yeah, those stumblebums. They might have

won if someone hadn't told Tucker he could hit. Why, he was a pitcher, not a hitter."

"Tie that one! Striking out with three on base. Gabby Spencer would have pulled his underwear off right out there on the field."

"Uhuh. I always said that boy was a false alarm. My dope is he never had anything the matter with his arm. Just yellow, that's all. Wonder why Leonard holds on to him."

That was enough. Eating was impossible. He paid his bill and rose. The waitress was distressed. Wasn't the meat good? Did he want to change it for something else? No, thanks, nope. The woman at the desk near the entrance looked at him queerly when he went out, and he hoped she didn't recognize him. At the drugstore they didn't. He stopped to buy some toothpowder, and heard the words:

"Why, that big palooka, whoever told him he could hit?"

"Yeah," rejoined the clerk as he wrapped up the toothpowder. "He couldn't hit a grapefruit, he couldn't. Useter be able to pitch, why, sure, but now he's just another one of the hired hands. Well . . . the Dodgers were always like that."

Beaten and discouraged, he sneaked back to the hotel, got through the lobby before any of the gang saw him, went up in the elevator and locked himself in his room. Already the September dusk was falling; soon night came on and the room blackened. He thought over the spring and summer, Clearwater, the wonderful game against the Yanks, the trip north, those early fights to lead the League with Gabby in there, nose to nose against the umpires, that great no-hit game against Cincinnati at night, and then —then, the push in the showers. Well, now it was over and finished; now he wanted one thing: home. He wanted to get home. He was sick and tired of baseball. He never wanted to see a ball park again as long as he lived. He was through, finished, done, he must get away as fast as he could. He'd ask Dave to release him the next morning. That would make things easier all round, and then he could take the first train for Hartford and home. He rose, turned on the lights, and started to pack.

It was a familiar knock, but it had something peremptory in it too.

"Come in."

Someone rattled the door. It was locked. The Kid opened it to find Dave. The manager entered, gave a quick look round the disordered room, the suitcases on the chairs, the piles of dirty clothes in the corner, and then glanced at the Kid who was removing one of the bags so his visitor could sit down.

"Have a seat, Dave. I'm glad you came. Wanted to say something to you."

The older man, his inevitable toothpick in his mouth, sat down, shaking his head. There was reproof in the gesture, but there was understanding in it, too.

"Now where you going?"

"Home."

"Home?" He didn't protest, he accepted the situation. "Are you really? Quitting, hey?" The toothpick did a dance across his mouth.

"No, I'm just a washout. I must get away."

There was a silence in the room. Somewhere

underneath the hotel the subway roared. The old ballplayer thought a minute before speaking. "Roy, I just come from Eddie Davis. He's down there in 916 crying his eyes out, 'cause he thinks he's through, like you. Point about that boy is, he came along too quick. Then he was given too much advice, everyone gave him advice, the coaches'n Gabby'n everyone else had to tell him how to play his position. He started missing hits he used to put in his pocket, then he tightened up, fell away in his hitting, and had to be yanked. There's been too much advice handed out on this ballclub. Now I told him, same as I told you, if he wants to make good it's up to him. And you."

The toothpick agitated itself up and down. "Listen to me. I can play bridge with a man and usually tell whether he'll be a ballplayer. If he has one thing. Remember what I told you that night back in Florida when you were sitting in the dark in your room sorry for yourself, remember? One thing, remember, courage. Has a guy got it?"

"But, Dave, I'm all washed up. I'm no good in the box; what use am I anyhow?"

"Suppose I quit like this last month when they gave me an unconditional release? You may say I had luck, getting back so soon. Sure, luck always comes to the tryers. Maybe you'll say you had tough luck. So you did. Now you find yourself on the spot. So'm I. A big-league manager is on the spot all the time. He's got to have plenty of what it takes. He's got to run a show of twenty-five prima donnas as different as you and Razzle Nugent. He must go out on the field, do the unexpected, and be willing to take punishment when the breaks go against his club. When the fans jeer and call him funny names." The Kid, sitting on the edge of the bed, shifted nervously, and Dave was quick to notice his movement. His toothpick rose rapidly up and down.

"Ha! So they got under your skin, hey? Why, boy, a manager has to take that every day in the week. When the situation calls for a bunt and he orders a hit-and-run and fails, he must be ready to take it on all sides. Gotta have courage. There's men on this team have nothing else but, like Jake, for instance. Has no life on his fast ball, a wrinkle for a curve, and nothing but slow and down and a bucketful of moxie. That's why he's still in there pitching winning ball at thirty-seven." He paused and removed the toothpick from one corner of his mouth to place it in the other corner.

"They got under your skin today, the fans out there, didn't they? You can't take it, hey? Trouble with you is, you're used to being Mr. Big. Had some luck, you did; lotta luck considering you had just a pretty fair country assortment. But you aren't used to the tough side. You were gonna whang that pineapple out of the park in the ninth, and what happened? You struck out. Then you go to pieces. Just like Eddie Davis. Can't take it. . . ." The toothpick started its quivering dance around his mouth, but the Kid stopped it short. He rose.

His face was flushed. He was angry. "Yeah . . . who says so?"

"Why, everyone. Boys on the club. The fans. Even you do. See, you admit it yourself." He pointed round the room at the suitcases, at the piles of clothes, at the half-opened drawers. "Cut and run this way; why, you can't take it. 'Course it was okay when things were going well, when you were a flash and a star and in every headline and the boys were giving you interviews and write-ups, all this Kid-from-Tomkinsville-stuff, it was fine back in June pitching shut-out ball. We were all fresh in June, yes, and good too. Not now. You can't take it. There's a saying down my way, Roy; maybe you heard it. I come from a great fishing country, and this is how they put it down there." He paused and so did the toothpick. The Kid, angry and annoyed, glanced up as he hesitated.

"Only the game fish swim upstream. Remember that, Roy, when you get back home." He repeated the phrase, turning it round and round in his mouth as the toothpick waggled in tune. "Only the . . . game fish . . . swim upstream. . . . Well"—he rose—"too bad you can't take it."

Now he was really mad. Now he was fighting mad. He was mad at old Dave for the first time.

"Can't I? Says who?"

"I do. Otherwise you'd stay right here and help out a losing ballclub."

The Kid suddenly stepped forward. He kicked a suitcase clean across the room. His big toe felt the effects of the blow for days afterward. "Dave, you just watch me. You'll see whether I can take it or not. . . ."

He turned his back and, leaning over, started to throw a mess of dirty laundry onto the floor

THE KID KICKED IT CLEAN ACROSS THE ROOM

of the closet. The door shut with a bang. He closed the drawers of the bureau and, catching up a suitcase, flung it back under the bed. Only . . . the game fish swim . . . upstream. . . .

16

Anyhow, he had his job back. That was something.

Curious, too, because he distinctly remembered old Mr. MacKenzie telling him in a sharp voice that he "wasn't keeping the place open for no ballplayers." There had been scorn in his tone as he mentioned the last word. Yet when the Kid returned it appeared Mr. MacKenzie had said nothing of the sort. Mr. MacKenzie had merely offered to take Jimmy Harrison on until his return. Whatever the facts, the Kid was now famous, and being in the drugstore again didn't hurt business. Folks came in all day long and stayed. They all knew him and all wanted to know things about the big leagues, and Gabby's death, and was it true what the newspapers said about Razzle Nugent, and did the Cubs have the best chance for next year, and was this boy Raynor of the Tigers really fast, and a hundred other silly questions. Naturally if they came and stayed, they had to buy something. Maybe Mr. MacKenzie was smart at that.

The Kid had no contract, no way of knowing

whether he'd get back on the team or any team anywhere the next season; nevertheless he was the town's hero. Had he not played big-time ball? Being the town's hero bothered him because he realized it was extremely likely he would never be called again, and would always be a guy who once played with the Dodgers. This he felt. But he did not act on that feeling. Quite the contrary; he pretended to himself he was sure to go back to baseball, and on this theory he planned his winter.

Grandma thought he was crazy. Anyone who managed to drive a sleigh up the snowy road on the ridge where the going was hard, and saw his device in the barn behind the house, thought he had lost his mind. It looked like a fence, a structure of boards about four inches wide and four feet high, on top of which he placed a baseball.

The ball was attached by a string so that when hit it flew away ten yards and bounced back. Standing at right angles to this board he could practice hitting alone.

By the time snow came the road was seldom plowed and he was unable to use his old car going down to work. This he liked. Baseball was part condition; it was speed, speed, speed, and a good deal of the speed was speed of foot. He had walked down before many times, but never run. Now he began running, a slow easy jog trot at first, then faster as he became used to the two and a half mile trip twice a day. The run back at eight-thirty after work in the dark with a cold wind and snowflakes whistling down the road was sometimes hard. But no matter what the temperature, he kept at it; no matter how stormy it was he found time every morning to go for his practice swings to tune up his hitting in the barn.

"Keep your bat level," Dave had said. That was it, that was the one important thing, keep his bat level. A tendency to keep his right shoulder down, to swing up, was his worst fault. If only that could be corrected, he might some day be a hitter. Standing before the little fence he was obliged to keep his bat level. If he didn't, if he dropped his bat two inches, he cracked the edge of the wood and almost stung his hands off. Joe and Harry Cousins, the twins who played end on the Luther Jackson High football team with him, and Jess Moore who lived on the farm down the road, often used to drop past and watch. Day after day they found him in the icy barn trying to shorten his stride as Dave had shown him, swinging his bat level. While they stood about in the cold winter air, stomping, rubbing their ears and clapping their hands, he kept steadily at it.

Step . . . swing . . . bat level . . . step . . . swing . . . step . . . swing . . . bat level . . . gosh, it's cold today . . . step . . . swing . . . must be five below . . . bat level . . . step . . . swing . . . keep that old bat level . . . step . . . swing . . . that . . . there, that was more like it . . . now . . . that was good, that was . . . now . . . step . . . swing . . . bat level. . . .

While Joe or Harry or Jess secured the ball as it bounced and dangled on the end of the string and placed it once again on top of the wooden barrier, Grandma, sympathetic and understanding at first, shook her head as he came in cold winter mornings wringing wet from his hitting that ball on the little fence. An hour, only one hour, but sixty minutes of continuous batting practice is a long, long while. Mighty tiring, too.

"Roy, you'll catch your death of cold if you keep on this way. When you have a good job, too, and Mr. MacKenzie such a real nice man. . . ."

The Kid wasn't so sure about Mr. MacKenzie. Business boomed all winter and he discovered that every day he had a constant stream of questions to answer no matter how often the questioners had been in before. Luckily they were the same questions so he could reply mechanically as he worked.

"Nosuh, ain't heard a thing yet. . . . Yessuh, they're a little late with contracts this year. . . . No'm, ballplayers are right good boys. . . . Hard work? You bet it's hard work. . . . Razzle Nugent? Oh, he's a great guy, he is. . . . No, Tommy, nothing yet. . . . Oh, mebbe they'll send me a contract, mebbe they won't. . . . You never know . . . just gotta wait. . . . Yessir, Gabby was a great ballplayer, lotta pepper, that's right. . . . Nosir, I wouldn't know if he was as good a shortstop as Honus Wagner. . . . Oh, yes, Mis' Kennison, guess I did have some bad luck; well, it's all in the game. . . . No, Mr. Hawkins, haven't heard anything yet. . . . Yessir, I sure am glad to have this job. Yessir, thank you very much, Grandma's fine. . . ."

It was a cold morning in early January when she heard a knock on the kitchen door, the only door in the house which Grandma allowed open in the winter. Wiping her hands on her apron, for she had been washing the breakfast dishes, she went across the room and opened the door to find Perley Peters, the rural delivery mail carrier. Perley wore his winter costume: a short sheepskin jacket, boots, and a fur cap. His ears were red and so was his nose.

"My goodness, Perley, you look like you was froze. Come right in; come in and have a cup of hot coffee."

"Thanks, don't mind if I do have something hot, Mis' Tucker. Cold out there on the ridge." There was a grin on his face which betrayed his interest in the Tucker family and the interest of all Tomkinsville in the boy who had carried the town onto the sports pages of the big city dailies.

"First of all . . ." He pulled off his fur glove and fumbled in the mail sack slung over his shoulder. "Mis' Tucker, looks like it's come at last. Registered, too."

"Goodness sakes alive!" She hoped and yet she didn't hope. She hoped for Roy. She knew his disappointment and how bitter it would be not to return to the game, but she didn't want him to go through another six months' strain like the summer before. Nor did she want to go through it again herself.

Perley peeled off his second glove and dug into the sack. There it was, attached by a rubber band and several clips to a small red card. They were careful all right, down in the post office.

"See. Brooklyn Baseball Club." Grandma searched in the pocket of her apron for her reading glasses. She realized as she took the letter

GRANDMA HELD THE LETTER IN HER HAND

that she was as excited as Roy possibly could be. Brooklyn Baseball Club, 215 Montague Street, Brooklyn, N. Y. "My goodness!" She held the letter in her hand as if it were gold, which indeed it was. "My goodness sakes alive. . . ."

"Yep. There 'tis. Now . . ." He pulled out the little red card from the envelope and handed it to her with a pencil. "Return receipt requested . . . sign there. . . ."

Grandma drew herself up.

"No. That letter's for Roy. Let him sign himself; he hasn't gone down to work yet. You'll find him out there practicing with that baseball contraption in the barn." The mailman put on his cap, buttoned his coat, drew on his gloves, and, taking the letter and the red card, moved toward the door. "Come back, Perley; I'll put some coffee on to heat."

Perley opened the door. As he did so a sharp noise entered the kitchen. It was the same noise heard all summer long in a thousand ball parks.

"Crack . . ." The clean sweet sound of a bat squarely meeting a ball.

Grandma stood, happy and yet not happy underneath. If only they wouldn't work him to the bone the way they did last summer. She started to put on the coffee, placed the pot on the stove, and removed her reading glasses. Then there was crunching of feet on the snowy pathway to the backyard, the door was swung open, and he burst into the room. In his hand was the opened letter and attached to it was a long green check.

"It's come, Grandma, it's come. . . ."

17

It was great to be back.

Hullo, Red, hullo, Karl, hullo, Doc, how are you, anyway, hullo, Ray, hullo, Eddie, hullo there, Fat Stuff, hullo, Jerry, hullo, Rats, hullo, Jake. . . .

Great to be back? You bet it was great to be back. Dave, accompanied by the pitching staff, plus Babe Stansworth and a couple of rookie catchers and the two coaches, Draper and Cassidy, had been limbering up for a couple of weeks at Hot Springs. They were all waiting at Clearwater, as the main group rolled in on various trains from the North and the West.

Great to be back? Sure was great. To see them all once more and feel they were glad to see him too; once more to be a part if only a small and unimportant part of that moving unit, a baseball club. Hullo, Harry, hullo, Tom, hullo, Razzle, hullo, Ed, hullo, Steve, hullo, Mr. Hanson.

Great to be back? Yes, it was wonderful. To eat on the roof of the Fort Harrison again, hearing the familiar chatter across the tables, and Razzle's voice addressing the waitress as "sweetmeat" and demanding more ice cream. Yes, it was great to see them all, to shake hands with old Chiselbeak in the locker room, who patted him heartily on the back and called him "boy." Great to be there, to watch the old man hand out uniforms and scold them as usual for not taking care of their stuff. The Kid was glad to see them, everyone down to little Snow White, the pickaninny who was their mascot and bat boy in Clearwater.

Great to be back, to be away from the cold and damp and slush of March on the ridge, away from that job with those everlasting questioners; great to feel the warm Florida sunshine once more on his face and neck, to hear the clack-clack, clackety-clack of spikes on the concrete of the clubhouse porch, to stand in the shower relieving tired muscles and listen to their talk.

"Who was that pitching in batting practice today, Frank—that big feller?"

"That? That was Roger Stinson; used to be with the Cubs. Whad'je do all winter, Jake—hunt? Say, what do you-all hunt in those North Carolina woods? Lions?"

"Nope. Squirrels. Just squirrels, that's all. I did plenty of squirrel hunting last winter."

Someone came in and threw himself on a bench. "Phew! I'm tired. Hey, there, Chiselbeak, gimme a Coke. Tired? Yeah, and you'd be tired too if you'd pitched for batting practice twenty minutes and then hit grounders to the infield thirty minutes on top of that!"

"You'd have been in fifteen minutes sooner if Red had only stopped a few."

"Yeah. I can make him look awful good or awful bad with that-there bat."

"Hey, Tucker . . . Roy . . . you got a new stance, haven't you . . . since last year?"

". . . and just lemme tell you one thing . . . He's good, that rookie is. He'll give Jerry a battle for his job, you see if he doesn't. Led off for Knoxville last summer. And has he power! Tells me he can play anywhere in the infield too."

"Say, Tom, did you see that lad Street today? He warmed up right-handed, and then when they played those three innings he went in and batted left-handed."

"Yeah. Bingo Murray was like that. He'd bat right-handed against the southpaws and left-handed against right-handers. That Street may do some hitting this year. Here comes Rats. Hey there, Rats old sock. What's the matter? Don't give him a Coke, Chiselbeak; the boys hit him out of the box. How come, Rats?"

"Oh . . . I dunno. I was wild. You know how it is the start of the season. Besides, the wind out there . . . it always blows down here in Florida. . . ." A guffaw rose from the showers.

"The wind! The wind, nuts! He's a lefty, ain't he?"

"You bet he's a lefty. Tha's why umpires wear shinguards."

Yes, it was great to be back. The long, tiring practice, those hours of punishment were now fun. The Kid loved it all, loved chasing fungoes in the outfield, loved the throwing to bases and the plate, loved most of all the batting practice. His hitting was truer, less spasmodic, and several players noticed it. One evening Dave came up to him in the lobby of the hotel.

"We'll start the first inter-club game tomorrow.

I'm using you at center field on the Yannigans. You boys will have Razzle to start, and then Jake and young Speed Boy Davis, this rookie from

Atlanta. I want to see what he really has. By the way, Roy, haven't you changed your batting stance?"

"Yes, I have, Dave. I practiced all winter, you know. Shortened my stride like you said."

The manager looked at him a minute. "I thought so. You're swinging level too. Least, you were every time I saw you this morning."

"I'm trying to, Dave. You know I like to hit."

He put his hand on the Kid's shoulder. "Remember what I always told you, Roy. Any kid who doesn't pull and isn't afraid'll be a good hitter. Don't you ever forget it."

Yes, it was great to be back. To be with them all again, to go out to practice and watch Dave on his hands behind the plate, hear him shout:

"All right now, squeeze play." It was a bunt down the third base line which he had to field to first or second, fast work, and fast work for the basemen too. There was the same speed and the same stress on speed as ever, but there was less pressure on the team because Dave's methods were different from Gabby's. He was less of a scrapper, less voluble, quieter; but he was in there every second, watching, missing nothing from his post of vantage behind the plate.

"Wait a minute. What's the matter with you fellas out there? You oughta run a man down on bases with two throws. If you chuck that ball round it gets hot. Now try it again. . . ."

Perhaps the thing which most heartened the Kid was the morning a robust, sandy-haired and freckle-faced man, in a loud sports jacket and a Panama over his eyes, joined them. He shook hands with everyone on the clubhouse porch, although the Kid didn't stop as he tromped past to the field for fear MacManus had forgotten him. Later in the morning the great man was sitting in a box and talking to Dave, who was standing below with a bat in his hand leaning against the rail. Roy had been in a pepper game and came near to chase a loose ball.

"Hey . . . Roy . . . Roy Tucker . . . how are you anyhow?"

The Kid picked up the ball and saw the great man smiling at him from the front box. His hand was stretched out. "Say, I'm glad to see you back." He said it as if he meant it. "Mighty glad to have you back. The old whip okay, is it?"

"Yessir. So long as I don't pitch, it's just fine. Doc Masters been all over it; says he thinks it'll hold up all right."

"Now, that's dandy. I'm glad to see you back 'cause you had some pretty tough luck last year. It's good to know they couldn't lick you; that's the kind of a fighting ballplayer we want on this man's club. Eh, Dave? . . ."

The old catcher looked at the Kid and the Kid looked at Dave.

"Yes, Mac, we're expecting him to be useful this season. We want a fighting ballclub and there's a place for everyone who can scrap."

The Kid walked back to the pepper game in a glow. No wonder everyone on the club was willing to work their heads off for a man like that, to pitch out of turn, to run wild on the bases, to take dangerous chances to win games. Fight? Sure, he'd fight. He'd show 'em. Naturally . . . there wasn't any chance of displacing Case or Swanson or Scudder, the three fielders, yet he hoped just what Dave had said: to be useful.

Going back to the pepper game he passed a short, perspiring chap in a white suit with a gray felt hat over his eyes. He was smoking a cigar, had a newspaper folded up under one arm, and his hand in his trousers pocket. Casey.

"Hullo...."

The little chap looked up, surprised, saw one of the team in uniform, and hastily replied:

"Hullo, how are ya? . . ." It was evident from his inquiring glance he had no idea to whom he was speaking. Ten months before, the chunky man had been writing columns about the Kid and calling him by his first name. Now he couldn't remember who he was.

"Hullo, Mac . . . hullo there, Dave." The sports-writer paused a second because he was out of breath from his dash across the field. He had news, and was anxious to convey it to MacManus himself, and first. "Say, Mac, the office just wired down, wants to know if you'll take that one!"

"What one?" The Irishman sat erect in his chair, alert and suspicious. He was suspicious of every newspaperman but especially of Casey. "If it's one of Murphy's cracks, I've nothing to say."

"Yeah, I know, but here's what he said about..."

"Don't care what he said. Tell him to mind his own business and let us mind ours, will you?"

"Sure, sure, I will, Mac. Only this is straight from their training camp. No fooling. He says the team which beats the Dodgers will win the pennant this year."

There was a moment or two of silence.

"He did?" MacManus was slightly puzzled. He knew his rival probably didn't mean it. And yet...

"Uhuh. He says the team that beats Brooklyn will win the pennant. Only he doesn't know which one of the seven it will be."

18

Different managers; different ways of running a ballclub. Gabby stressed fight. Fight and discipline. You had to do what Gabby said, and like it. Every member of the club had to be in his room in the hotel at eleven and answer when old Chiselbeak made the rounds and knocked on every door. Dave abolished this. He stressed one thing: initiative. Each man was to live sensibly, to do his own thinking on the field. For instance, signal-stealing, a pastime of Gabby's which Charlie Draper, the third base coach, had developed into an art, was abandoned. As a catcher Dave knew far too much about mixing signals to feel they did you much good even when you knew them.

"I was on the old Senators back in the '33 Series, and Monte Davis stole all the Giants' signals. What good did it do us? We couldn't lick 'em. Any first-class catcher can mix up signs so that wiseacre out there on second will be crossed up. If he signs in a fast ball and the pitcher serves a hook—well, you know the answer. That's one reason you don't find Scrapper Knight or the good hitters taking information. I want this club to play heads-up, percentage ball; most of all I want them to do their own thinking out there, not be relying on someone handing them the signals. . . ."

But if signal-stealing was out, much of the raucous spirit which Gabby had instilled into the club stuck. They were still a noisy, fighting team, they still got on with umpires like a family of wildcats, were still cordially disliked by those gentlemen and respected if not feared by all adversaries, even though they had finished the previous season in sixth place. Gabby's pep and ginger was not entirely lacking, either, for Harry Street at short turned out to be an acceptable replacement. Confidence? He had it, a-plenty. Pep? Fight? He was full of it. His eternal chatter, his everlasting slogan: "Hurry up there . . . take your time . . ." rang out over the diamond from the field or bench every day. At first the team and especially the older players, save the Kid, his roommate who knew him best, disliked him; to them he was still "that fresh young busher at short." Then during the pre-season training camp games they began to admit grudgingly the youngster had something. Afraid of nothing, Harry was making stops back of second Gabby would never have touched. In the early stages he led the squad in hitting. Before long everyone had an opportunity to see that he could turn the heat on the enemy also. It was during the trip north when the Dodgers were playing one-night stands with the Detroit Tigers that young "Childe Harold," as the sportswriters named him, stunned both teams.

Harry believed the bigger they are the harder they fall. So he turned his attention to the biggest thing at hand, Scrapper Knight, the great Tiger star who for six years had led the American League in batting, and after a long career was slowly nearing his end as a big-time player. The terror of pitchers, he was also the terror of fielders on the basepaths because more than one of them carried Scrapper's initials carved on shinbones or hips. In the first game of the series, with the score three to one for Brooklyn in the fifth, Scrapper singled and the next man slapped a beautiful low line drive to Karl Case in right. The Tiger star, with a generous lead off first, saw it wasn't going to be caught and, as was his habit, tried for third. Passing second, Harry gave him the hip, not crudely enough to attract the attention of the umpires, but sufficiently to throw him out of his stride so he was cut down by two feet at third base. When the two teams changed sides, Scrapper walked over. He was boiling mad.

"The next time you try that, you fresh young busher, I'll cut your legs off."

Harry stood holding his ground. Chin to chin he looked the great man in the eye.

"You'll cut nothing," he said coldly but distinctly. "You been bulldozing guys on second for years, but you can't pull that stuff on me. Next time you come round I won't be so careful; I'll spill you on your ugly old face."

For almost the first time Scrapper was speechless. Players didn't talk back to Scrapper, let alone fresh rookies; they had respect for him. He was dangerous. He was the star batter of the League. He was Scrapper Knight, the great

Scrapper. Now everyone had heard the boy's rejoinder, old Stubblebeard the umpire, several members of the Dodgers, as well as four or five Tigers who gathered about to watch Scrapper carve the youngster up. They all stood transfixed.

While the veteran was struggling in his throat for words, the boy suddenly broke in again:

"Listen, Scrapper. Everyone knows you're through. Why don't you turn in that uniform and give yourself up?"

The big fellow heard for the first time the sentence he had been dreading for months and months, words that no one had yet dared say to him, words he knew in his heart, knew in his legs where it counted, were true. He, Scrapper the great, was almost through. The young blighter was right. He looked, glared, hesitated, started to throw a punch at the boy's chin . . . and then turned away. That was all. There wasn't any more. But from that moment even the veterans on the Dodgers respected this amazing youngster.

The previous season during the early games, Roy had been making a name for himself on the mound, while Harry sat in the dugout watching Gabby cavort round short. This year their situation was reversed. Harry was out there playing, while except as an occasional pinch hitter, a role he didn't much enjoy because of what was at stake, the Kid saw little service as the team moved north. He warmed the bench, eating peanuts and listening to Dave. Learned things, he did, too. Especially about defensive strategy for, as he began to realize, Dave was one of the real

HARRY STOOD HOLDING HIS GROUND

strategists of the game. Casey and other sportswriters had hinted during the winter and spring that Dave would try to do the catching, that Babe Stansworth, the regular catcher and a .325 hitter, would be exchanged for a sadly needed pitcher now Dave was back. Nothing of the sort occurred.

Although he took his turn behind the plate occasionally, Dave let Babe continue as first string catcher, but he never let him or anyone forget who was running things. If the new manager was less pointed in his comments than Gabby, and if he did no sensational master-minding, he had definite ideas and ran his own show with a fine sense of where to place men and what to do under every circumstance, for he knew the hitters better than anyone in the game. Gradually the Kid saw the field as a checkerboard where each man on the club was at a certain place on a certain play; slowly he observed things that as a pitcher he had never seen, or more likely seen a hundred times and always taken for granted without thinking. How, for instance, the fielders studied the batters, or how Dave waved them from side to side, in or out, with the scorecard in his hand as different hitters stepped to the plate. How outfielders watched the wind currents and judged plays accordingly, how when two men were able to catch a fly the one who took it was always the one the catch left in a throwing position. These and dozens of other things the Kid realized, sitting there on the bench in half a dozen cities between Clearwater and Brooklyn.

They started the season playing well. As Casey remarked in his column one morning, the Dodgers always started playing well. They could be counted to be up front in May and well to the bottom in September. Dave shut his lips when he read this but said nothing. By the end of the first month, as Casey had predicted, the team was in third place, playing snappy ball. But they still needed one first-class pitcher to fill the place left vacant by the Kid. None of the new men proved reliable, while the regulars were all a year older. Dave knew this. So did MacManus who spent hours and hours in planes and trains looking over likely prospects. One deal he wanted to make was for Elmer McCaffrey, a southpaw who had won sixteen games for the last place Phillies the previous season. But this was blocked because the Phils wanted money; plenty of it, plus a couple of players.

Then on their second western trip in June it happened. Casey expressed his opinion of Mac's intelligence in this vein:

"You can always depend on the Dodgers. If it isn't injuries, or sickness, or accidents—you remember Gabby Gus Spencer wrapped his car round a telegraph pole last summer—it's the humidity. Must have been the humidity which went to the head of Laughing Jack MacManus, the Dodger owner, this week. You got to hand it to Jack. He shocks the daylights out of his rivals, pulls off night baseball with its didoes, and all in all is the most refreshing thing in the big leagues since the first bounce was out. But his recent trade of Joe Gunther, the sensational young rookie infielder from Baltimore, and Tommy Scudder, who just now tops the league left fielders at the plate, plus $15,000 cash for Elmer McCaffrey, Philadelphia left-hander, is just one of those things which make folks wonder about Mac's sanity.

"If his team isn't in trouble, trust Jack to stick his handsome Irish phiz into things and manufacture trouble. Breaking up his outfield combination, about all the Dodgers ever had, is one thing. Signing Elmer McCaffrey is something else again. Elmer is a good country pitcher who may win ten games for the Flatbush Flounders, but in exchange Mac gave up a cog in the fastest and best-hitting outfield in either league, plus a youngster who showed plenty last spring down in Clearwater.

"Manager Dave Leonard now reports that he expects to move Karl Case over to left and put Roy Tucker in right. You remember Roy, the Kid from Tomkinsville, who after winning fifteen straight games in the box last summer had the misfortune—only a Dodger could do it—to fall in the showers and chip his elbow bone so he couldn't pitch any more. Roy is an early-to-bed, early-to-rise, small town boy. Always in shape, winter or summer, he's one of those earnest types taking voluntary batting practice every morning on the hottest days of summer. He seldom opens his trap except to say something pleasant, and the umpires all like him, about the only member of the club they do, because he never squawks. So far he's never been put out of a single game. It's too bad MacManus is losing his head, but there doesn't seem to be anything we can do about it.

"Mac, you don't win pennants with nice, soft-speaking, early-to-bed home town boys out there in right field."

19

Everything was upside down. Now he saw things from the other side.

Once he loved the "Airport" as the boys called Braves Field in Boston, one of the biggest parks in the League and a pitcher's paradise because outfielders had plenty of room to roam about and pull down hits that would have been homers in Brooklyn. All a pitcher had to do in Boston was get the ball over. Whereas the Polo Grounds, where a man could get a "Chinese home run" by merely hitting 257 feet over the right field fence, was a nightmare. Now things were reversed. Now he saw the game from the batter's point of view.

Yet he hadn't completely forgotten what he'd learned from Dave as a pitcher, and it was a help. He knew exactly how the wind currents would affect different hitters and how the man in the box would throw to them; knew when a low curve was coming to bait the batter, and when the pitcher would keep the ball high. This enabled him to take chances, for he knew the men pitching also. He was able to anticipate drives and catch balls other fielders stretched for in vain; he was fast enough to cut off many balls that most fielders would have let by, and he soon learned how a squarely hit line drive turned into a sinker when it came to the man in the field. Before long he was making the fans at Ebbets Field forget Tommy Scudder. Especially at the plate.

His winter's work and his morning batting practice which he kept up steadily had their effect. At first Dave had placed him in the seventh slot just above Jerry Strong, the weakest hitter on the club, and the pitcher, but you couldn't keep a man who was punching the ball steadily into left field and hitting homers all over the short fences in the League in the seventh spot. So he was moved up to second. It was lucky he liked to hit. Lucky too that he had always been willing in practice to go out and shag flies and throw in to the plate. All this helped him in his new position.

Naturally at first everyone tried to steal on him or pick up an extra base and stretch hits. They soon quit. Because they saw that the Kid was as fast as any outfielder in the business and that his throwing was far more accurate than most. Instead of taking chances, they discovered they were out if they risked his arm, and he began to hold hits that were two baggers to a single base. Casey was still dubious about the Kid as a permanent fixture in right field but other sportswriters went all out, and Rex King of the *Times* remarked, as his home run total rose with the Dodgers' standing in the League:

"Some of the best pitchers imagined that because he had once been a member of the fraternity our Mr. Tucker would be duck soup at the plate. Nothing of the sort. Roy was never a bad hitter and nowadays hurlers who take nicely calculated dusters at his noggin live to regret it. The fact is that this lad can really hit. Yesterday at Ebbets Field with the score tied in the ninth against the Cubs and the winning run on third, Spike Coffman threw his duster at the Kid's head and knocked him down. He got up, stepped into the box, and whistled the next pitch past Spike's ears for two bases to win the game. He does much more harm out there at the plate with his old bat than some of the more pugnacious members of the club used to do with their fists. Up in third place, this ballclub certainly isn't the same old Dodgers."

On the other hand, Casey, the perpetual skeptic, was doubtful. For some time he refused persistently to boost them even when they broke through in second place in late July. They'd been up there last year this time, hadn't they? What happened? They slumped. They'd slump again. It was inevitable. But the team was going well, pitchers were turning in good performances with regularity, Razzle won eight straight, and McCaffrey, with the Dodger infield dancing behind him, won five straight. That infield was something to watch, and Harry Street, besides being the second leading hitter in the League, was playing great ball around short.

As for Roy, he loved it. He was happy to be back with the team, happier still when his chance came to play, and, after a season in the box, the outfield position was easy. Before long he became at home in right field, became used to the strangeness of it, the nearness of the fans, not to mention their eccentricities in various cities. There was the queer old lady in St. Louis, who sat in the bleachers to whinny all through each game like a prize percheron. In Pittsburgh, a man with a tremendous bellow invariably sat in a box behind the Pirate dugout roaring with a zest that sent other occupants scurrying away whenever he sounded forth. But the worst of all was Al the Milkman.

Al was reputed to be one of the wealthiest citizens in Cincinnati. However, he liked to go out to Crosley Field and sit in the bleachers close to right field, wielding an enormous cowbell. Whenever the visiting players, and especially the right fielder, tried to make a catch or stop a difficult ball, Al would sound that cowbell as the ball descended.

It was in Cincinnati that the Kid let the bleachers bother him. Al took a fiendish pleasure in riding young players, and he had a genius for tormenting them at close range. By the aid of a megaphone he advised the Kid in loud tones to return to the box, informing him as he trotted past between innings that Leonard ought to put a real fielder in right, not a has-been pitcher. In one critical game against the Reds the Kid muffed a hard ground ball through his legs to the accompaniment of that infernal cowbell. Later on in August the team moved once more into Cincinnati, tied with the Reds for second, the Giants six games in the lead.

The day was torturingly hot, the game close, nerves were edgy with second place in the balance, and out in the right field bleachers Al the

Milkman was more raucous than ever. The Dodgers with Razzle in the box led two to one in the eighth and Cincinnati had a man on third with two out when the batter hit a high foul close to the right field bleachers where Al was sitting. As the Kid ran over, his tormentor rose, whanging his cowbell violently. Roy sighted the ball, heard the noise, knew he was getting closer and closer to the stands, looked up, got his hands on the foul . . . stumbled . . . and dropped it.

The crowd rose, Al jeering with the rest. Back walked Roy, ruefully thinking that a hit now might mean the game and second place. All because of that error. Again the batter poked a long fly to right, once more clearly foul. The Kid ran across again as Al resolutely mounted his chair, furiously swinging his bell. Roy instantly saw the ball was going into the stands about halfway up and near his persecutor.

"Take off your hat!" he shouted.

Standing in his seat, the cowbell waving, Al removed his straw hat with a flourish of delight, just in time to receive the ball on his shiny bald pate, a blow which knocked him over and out. They had to carry him from the stands, the cowbell silenced. Never again was the Kid bothered in Cincinnati.

On the bases he was fast, and a useful man to have on first with Allen or Street coming up and a hit-and-run on the cards. He liked running wild on the bases, took chances and more often than not got away with them. Except against big Muscles Mulligan, of the Giants. For some reason the New York first basemen took a fierce dislike to him, was always giving him the hip, or plank-

HIS TORMENTOR ROSE WHANGING HIS COWBELL

ing the ball on his ribs with more than ordinary fervor. Whenever the Kid made a long hit deep to the outfield, Muscles invariably tried to slow him up rounding first. Roy wanted to be friendly but the Giant infielder took it as a sign of weakness. Other tactics were necessary.

The Kid got even with him by stealing second or drawing throws from Muscles whenever possible. One day as he went to third on an infield grounder, an idea came. It was merely an idea, a thought in which a situation might develop where he could make Mulligan look foolish. So he made a dive for home and as the Giant first baseman drew his arm to throw, the Kid scrambled back to safety at third again. Time after time, when the same play came up, the Kid repeated the act, hoping some day to catch Muscles napping.

Meanwhile opposing pitchers began to take notice of him. He made them. "What shall we do with this bird Tucker? Give him a base on balls or play the outfielders the other side of the fence? Notice he got his sixteenth homer yesterday—that ties him with Buck Masterson."

"He sure can paste that old persimmon. But you can get him on a low ball if you use it right. No one can throw a fast ball past him. First time I threw a curve breaking outside, figuring to fool him. He took it for a strike. Then I came inside high which was a ball. That guy knows too much for his own good. The next was high inside but just over the plate for strike two. Then I slipped one low inside . . . and by gosh . . . he took it. . . ."

All this time the Dodger bench before the

game was a cheery spot. The team was in second place by a good margin, better still it was loose and chattering. To hear them no one would suspect they were closing in on the pace-setting Giants.

"I'm sitting there with a glass of beer in my hand . . ." It was Razzle sounding off.

"Where's Harry Street?"

"Must be down at the other end of the dugout, talking. We got Razzle up here."

"Whew, boy, it is sure hot out there."

"Aw, you guys haven't any idea of heat. When I was with the Browns we played thirty days in St. Louis when it was over 100 each day. That's equal to 120 degrees any other place."

"Well, as I was saying, I'm sitting there with a beer in my hand . . ."

"Hey, Mike . . . what do you weigh?"

" 'Bout 180. I go down to 170 after a game."

"Say, old Gabby could have pepped up those Cubs, couldn't he? Yes, sir, he'd have plugged that there hole at short all right."

"Well, I was with Chambersburg in the Blue Ridge League this year, and I'm sitting in the hotel with a glass beer in my hand, when . . ."

"Who's umpiring next week at the Polo Grounds? I hope Donahoe and Hines don't follow us over to New York."

"I'm sure glad they called that game in the rain yesterday. The way Liebert hit that ball past the 450 foot sign his first time up looked like he might break the game open if it went on much longer. Don't know how Tuck ever got it at all. That ball had more feathers on it than any ball I ever saw."

"Yep, the Kid can sure hound that old apple, Roy can."

"Hey, Jerry, how about a movie tonight?"

"Yeah. Okay, who's pitching for them?"

"See . . . it was like this. I'm sitting there in the hotel with a beer in my hand . . ."

"Wainwright? He's poison for me."

"Aw, he hasn't got so much. No live fast ball, but I tell ya he has a good knuckle ball and a swell change of pace. You gotta watch yourself."

"Hey, Red, see Casey's column today? He says

with the Dodgers in second place in August they ought to be given the saliva test. He says . . ."

"Aw, nuts to him. That wise guy."

As usual, Razzle had the last word. Almost.

"Well, as I was saying, I'm sitting in this-here-now hotel in Chambersburg with a glass beer in my hand when in walks this fella . . ."

Clang-clang. Clang-clang.

"Hey, Razzle, get out there. What d'you think they're paying you for on this club, to hear yourself talk?"

20

All right, Raz old boy, two down. . . ."
"Two down, everyone, two down."
"Attaboy, Raz, tha's chucking, that is. . . ."
"Hurry up, Razzle, take your time." Harry's everlasting war cry came from the other side of second. Leading the Giants three to two in the sixth, the team was confident and on its toes. Before the Kid was a scene he had been looking at every day for over two months: directly in front the broad, thick back of Red Allen, his hands on his knees; to the Kid's right the tall, lithe figure of Eddie leaning over characteristically to scoop dirt from the basepaths; beyond, Harry shouting his tag line, and further along dark-faced Jerry Strong near third. Razzle was in the box and Babe Stansworth, whose hitting had been such a factor in their rush ahead, was in his familiar crouch behind the plate. A scene he knew by heart.

Crack!

A slow roller to the left of the box, another easy out. The Kid could see Razzle going across, leaning down . . . and then suddenly straighten up while the ball hopped past untouched and the batter reached first.

The big pitcher hopped up and down on one foot and limped toward first. In a second he was surrounded. Red and Eddie and Harry Street rushed over; Babe came out from the plate, while Dave, followed by Doc Masters, scurried from the shelter of the bench.

The Doc, with his black bag beside him on the ground, bent over and felt gingerly of Razzle's left calf. A Charley horse. The pitcher with his arm on the Doc's shoulder limped to the dugout, his face twisted in pain, and, as he approached, threw his glove with disgust onto the bench. There was a hushed silence over the stands. Razzle's hurt himself! The players looked uncomfortably at each other while Fat Stuff came in from the bullpen and started warming up.

Things happen fast in baseball. On the second pitch Maguire, the Giant lead-off man, took a belt at the ball and gave it a ride over that short right field fence. Two runs in! As if it wasn't enough to lose old Razzle in this critical moment of the pennant race, they were also going to drop a vital game. Going into the ninth one run behind, the first Dodger batter struck out, and then McCaffrey, a good hitter in the pinches, was sent in for Fat Stuff. He received his base on balls and, as Swanson came up, made the sort of play that looks good when it comes off and awfully bad when it doesn't. Anyhow it was foolhardy base running. Swanny hit a slow grounder to short and McCaffrey, with a desperate effort, slid into the second baseman in an attempt to break up a doubleplay. He succeeded.

RAZZLE LIMPED TO THE DUGOUT

He also succeeded in wrenching his back so badly he had to be carried from the field.

Roy came to the plate. On the first pitch, a strike, Swanson was off for second, and made it. Two out and the tying run on second. A hit would do the trick, keep them in the ball game, and possibly bring victory. The Kid felt he never had wanted a hit as much as he did that minute, but his very desire seemed to tighten him up. He struck out and the game was over. Muscles had to put in his two cents' worth as he passed the Dodger dugout on the way to the showers. He called out in a taunting tone:

"Same old Dodgers." No one had the heart to take him up.

This triple blow came at a hot psychological moment. The Giants were staggering from the strain of setting the pace all summer while the Dodgers were afire. To lose the lead, lose the game, lose Razzle and McCaffrey, their two best pitchers, all in one afternoon was bad. Then the next day Harry Street was struck in the face by a thrown ball in practice, and was left behind when the team entrained that night for Boston to have X rays determine whether his jaw was fractured. In Boston the club faced two double-headers and a single game in three days with their two best pitchers and the star shortstop out of the line-up.

In the meantime Roy, for some inexplicable reason, found himself in a batting slump. After being up with the leading hitters, second in home runs in the League, he went for three straight games without a hit. No reason; it just happened. His slump, however, threw a responsibility on Red Allen, the next hitter, who soon found himself asked to carry an unequal share of the load. His batting fell off as well. The team won the second game of the opening doubleheader with Jake Kennedy pitching shut-out ball, but lost the other four. Bad weather, cold blasts, fog, a young Boston southpaw rookie, spike wounds received by Tommy Swanson, and a final defeat in thirteen innings, made the Dodgers miserable as they entrained for Chicago. They were now four full games behind the Giants and tied with Cincinnati and the Cubs for second place.

The club became jittery and dropped two more games in Chicago. The train was late and they arrived at La Salle Street Station only an hour before the opener. Then there was the letdown after that series in Boston, and the team was affected, Roy most of all. Everyone offered him advice. He was a switch hitter, so why not try the other side. Naturally left-handed, he practiced hitting from the other side of the plate and in the first game in Chicago went up from the right. No luck. It was his eighth game in succession without a hit. The Cubs who were enjoying themselves at the expense of the Dodgers were delighted.

"See you boys got a new .400 hitter on your club," remarked Sam Graff, the Chicago coach, to Charlie Draper on the third base line.

"Yeah!" Charlie knew Graff and was hesitant. "Yeah . . . whozat?"

"This Kid, now, young Tucker."

"Tucker! Hasn't made a hit in . . ."

"That's just it. He's a .400 hitter, or somewhere about there; hits .200 batting left-handed and .200 hitting right-handed." Sam roared at his wisecrack. It wasn't so terribly funny to the Dodgers and especially to the Kid who heard it all over the park. A .400 hitter!

His teammates all had suggestions to make about the slump. Karl Case, for instance, thought it was his stance.

"I was with Cleveland in '34 hitting .365 and led the League on doubles, then I went fifty-six times without a hit. . . ."

"Gosh!" The Kid was staggered. Fifty-six time at bat without a hit. Maybe he had thirty or more trips at the plate to go.

"Yessir. Fifty-six. That's right. I was hitting 'em all to center and then I changed my stance and shook out of it. Why don't you try that?"

But no change had any effect whatever. By this time the whole club was in a slump. From second they went down to third place and within a game and a half of fourth. Dave shook up the batting order, putting the Kid back to fifth and shoving Babe Stansworth into the second spot. But the jinx was riding. When the jinx is riding a ballclub it doesn't matter what the manager does or who plays or how the batting order is shifted. Regulars like Razzle and Harry Street were injured, replacements were thrown in, and then the replacements were injured also. Tony Kapura, a likely rookie from Minneapolis, fractured his ankle the second game he played, and then the usually mild and soft-spoken Fat Stuff, his nerves on edge from overwork, got into a dispute with old Hines, the umpire, and was suspended for two weeks with a $50 fine slapped on. Everything went wrong: hitting slump, injuries, suspensions. It was all part of baseball.

There was one bright spot. That was Dave. When the team was going well, Gabby was a marvelous leader, snapping everyone up in the field, keeping them on their toes and acting as a spur when they became complacent. But in a slump his nerves betrayed him. He tightened up and tended to help everyone else do exactly the same thing.

Whereas Dave's assets, his quietness, his patience and understanding, were an enormous help as the team looked at trouble. Dave was able to handle the players as individuals, treating each man differently. There was nothing hasty or panicky about him or his methods. True, he lacked the zip and fire of Gabby, there was none of the old college-try atmosphere about the dressing room after a victory, but in such a crisis as they were going through Dave could get more mileage out of a talk or a few words than Gabby or most managers could get from an hour's bawling-out. If he had to pan someone, Dave was always careful not to do it in the heat of the dressing room where everyone knew about the lecture, but alone in the evening when tempers had cooled off and there was no one round to listen. These men had served him faithfully, they were all doing their best, and he let them know they had time to right themselves as things broke badly. They were given every chance to regain their stride, and as far as their jobs were concerned both Dave and MacManus made them feel they still had everyone's confidence.

Most of all, as an old catcher Dave was wonderful with those temperamental artists, the pitchers. The Dodgers, like most teams, were as good as their pitchers, but with Fat Stuff out, Razzle and McCaffrey injured, the work fell on relief pitchers and two newcomers, Davison and Lester. He was asking them for extra duty; they responded with the best they had.

Once again, and not for the last time, Roy felt the speed of baseball. Speed, speed, speed. It was Clearwater. It was spring. Then all at once it was late August; it was almost fall. Time passed, a dizzy series of games in a twenty-eight-day heat wave, with sudden visions of hotel rooms so hot and so lifeless they were like prison cells, of burning afternoons in the outfields of St. Louis, Pittsburgh, and Cincinnati, of sleepless nights in Pullmans, of a jumbled mass of plays in games won and lost. Early in September things got worse. Each time he came up without a hit made it harder the next time, until the tension began to choke him up. I gotta get a hit, I gotta get a hit, gotta get a hit, he'd say to himself, and then walk up and pop up to the shortstop. Finally Dave pulled him out and put young Paul Roth, a substitute outfielder, in his place.

He was benched! Still the Kid persisted in his batting practice every morning. One day in Philadelphia he saw Dave standing beside him. A minute later the manager spoke in his ear and asked him to come up to the room that night. When he got there he found a worried Dave, and for the first time he noticed new lines over the manager's forehead. The strain was telling on him like everyone else.

"Roy, sit down, boy. I'm sorry about the slump; you've been choking up, but it won't last forever."

"I can't figure it out, Dave. I've changed my stance and it didn't do a bit of good. Tried everything, been out swinging every morning. . . ."

"Maybe you tried too much. Let me tell you what I think your trouble is. You haven't been playing for Brooklyn the last month."

"Not playing for Brooklyn?"

"Nope. You were playing for Roy Tucker."

"For Tucker?"

"Right. You weren't playing for this team. I'll explain what I mean. Those sixteen—seventeen—how many was it—those home runs you made were about the worst thing that ever happened to you. Point is, when you began to close in on old Masterson you saw yourself in a flash leading this-here League in homers. The Kid from Tomkinsville. Another Joe DiMag, hey? Thought you were anyhow. You got homers on the brain. . . ."

He protested, "No, no, that isn't so, Dave; that isn't true. . . ."

"You didn't even know it, didn't realize it maybe, but it's true. You forgot that you were playing for Brooklyn and started playing for Tucker. You became—now what was it the sportswriters called you . . . oh, yes, 'Bad News Tucker!' I saw you that afternoon last month at home when the cameramen all gathered round the plate as you came over with your sixteenth home run, and I saw those kids chasing you for your autograph after the game. Why, the answer's easy. You just forgot the team, Roy. That's why I had to bench you."

He started to reply, to say it was false, but the words stuck. He'd never thought those things actively, but they were all true and he knew it.

"Now first of all, Roy, quit worrying. That's what's the matter with this whole team now. When you aren't hitting, all pitchers look good to you, awfully good. Your confidence and timing is all shot to pieces. Oh, I know, I've had it happen to me, more than once. The pitcher you always thought you owned can make a monkey of you. Stop thinking about it, don't let it get under your skin. Next, remember that in this-here game they pay off not on homers, not even on your batting average either, but on one thing: your ability to bat in runs. Baseball's a team game and don't ever forget it.

"Here's something practical. About your hitting, I mean. Trouble is you've tightened up, and every time you step in there you're as tight as a steel rod. Lemme give you a tip. When you walk to the plate start whistling. What? Oh, anything at all . . . whistle *Yankee Doodle* and it will loosen you up. Then wade in and smack the first good one. Try it and see. Now, boy, go downstairs and have a couple of beers, and then get on up to bed and forget it. Good night."

21

Hopelessly entrenched in fourth place in the first week in September, the Dodgers watched the bitter struggle for second between the Cubs and the Cards. Up front were the Giants with a four game lead, not much but safe unless the second place team suddenly became hot. In the American League the Yanks as usual were far out in front, and as Casey put it:

"The Dodgers in fourth place are so far behind these days they are calling in their farm hands. The Yanks are so far ahead they are calling in their outfield. With three weeks of the season to go both races seem settled and it looks like another five cent World Series."

It was true that Dave had called in some of the likely youngsters from farm teams for try-outs. This fact, added to the approaching end of the season, turned the squad to looking ahead, wondering about jobs for next summer and how the recruits would shape up in trying for their positions. Most of the men who had played through the year were not unhappy about their work. Last season they had risen from last place to sixth, and except for the slump caused by bad luck and unexpected injuries, they might now be in second or third. Next year. It was the ancient Brooklyn war cry. Next year . . . next year . . . next year. . . .

Dave heard it. He heard the words in the dugout, in the showers, in the hotel lobby, and at meals. With two and a half weeks to go the Dodgers were three games behind third place and seven back of second. But if some of the players were contented and had already counted themselves out for the season, he had not. Just as the squad was ready to take the field the next afternoon he came into the dressing room with MacManus on his heels. The Kid felt something was about to happen.

It was not a hunch because he saw Dave's face. The veteran catcher had grown older during the wearing summer months; streaks of gray were noticeable over his ears, and there were new lines around his mouth and in his forehead. The strain was telling. When he saw Dave enter the room with a tight look on his face, Roy knew something was going to burst. For whereas Gabby's fight talks were frequent and impressive, Dave handled the team individually, seldom talking to them as a group. Something important was therefore in the cards, this the Kid knew by the expression on the manager's face, by the serious look on the freckled countenance of MacManus as he closed the door leading to the office. Dave's face was serious too; he hitched at his belt, put one leg up on a bench before his locker, and leaned over on his knee. Just behind stood MacManus nervously lighting a cigarette, and Bill

DAVE'S FACE WAS SERIOUS

Hanson, the business manager, peered over the heads from a distant corner. The whole family; behind the circle fluttered old Chiselbeak, his arms full of dirty clothes.

Dave looked around. At the men with their arms on each other's shoulders. At those standing expectantly in front of their lockers, arms on their hips, at the four or five seated cross-legged on the floor. He waited until silence covered them. It was an impressive silence. Something was certainly coming.

"Been hearing talk these past few days . . ." He paused a moment. His start was direct, to the point, like Dave. Then he snapped out the next words.

"About next year!" Everyone instantly straightened up. It was strange how every man was affected. Gabby's pep talks were accepted, listened to, even heeded sometimes, but this was different. Those words cut. Someone's feet scuffled nervously on the floor, and a pair of spikes in the back of the room made a noise. Here and there a man shifted the gum in his mouth and swallowed, and hasty glances were shot across the circle. This hurt. This was a new Dave, stern-faced, frowning, terse.

"Now just one thing . . . and get this straight, every one of you. I'm not interested in next year. Is that clear? Neither is Mac. We're interested in this year, right now, today. If anyone doesn't get me, if there's any man on the squad not anxious to give his best this minute, he better take off his uniform, step in at the office, and get his paycheck. Hanson's here; he'll be glad to give you an unconditional release."

The short sentences of the old player hurt, they cut into every man, into the veterans of a dozen campaigns like Jake and Fat Stuff, into the youngsters like the Kid and Harry Street, into the irrepressible rookies from the minors. There was silence before, but it was nothing to the silence now. Scowling, MacManus flipped away his cigarette which sounded like lead as it bounced along the floor. Yes, this was a new, a different Dave, and the gang began to appreciate that anyone who imagined he lacked Gabby's force and fire was vastly mistaken. This was the boss. The boss was talking.

"Tuesday, Fat Stuff will be ready. Razzle is back today and Doc says he can pitch this week. Street goes in there this afternoon. McCaffrey returns tomorrow or Thursday. In four-five days we'll be at full strength again, or something like. Now this is almost the end of this season. Lots of you are banged up. I know it. Lots of you have bum arms or legs, razzberries or spike wounds. I know it. Everyone is down pretty fine. All right, so what? So are the Cubs, so are the Cards. Only difference is they're still in there fighting. They aren't talking 'bout next year.

"Yes, we've been in a slump. That comes to the best of clubs; no one can help it. I understand, been through plenty of 'em in my time. I can make allowances for that, for men who are trying just the same. One player hasn't been hitting and I had to bench him, but he's still out there taking his crack at batting practice every morning. You all know who that is. He's not talking about next year, he's trying hard to find himself this year, right now. I think he will, too;

I got confidence in him. Some of you pitchers complain you been overworked. I know it as well as you do. This week we ought to be back to a normal schedule again, with Raz and McCaffrey in the line-up. No one can help these things. But you can help this next-year attitude you got into lately. A team that looks to next year is a team that has quit. I want a fighting team on that field until the last out on the last afternoon. Get me; the last out . . . on the last afternoon. That's when the season ends."

He glanced over the men, at their tanned, solemn faces.

"Snap out of it, you guys. Forget next year, or you'll find that little pink slip in your mailbox tomorrow morning. Today we're in fourth place. We won't stay there unless we keep fighting and we needn't stay there if we do, either. All right; line-up for today:

"Swanny, center. Tucker, right. Red, first. Street, short. Stansworth behind the bat. Case, left. Davis, second. Strong, third. Kennedy in the box. That's all." There was a second or two when, stupefied by the fire of this usually mild and comradely man, they hesitated. Then they turned toward the door.

"Wait a minute! One thing more. There's some teams can count on their opponents losing; the Yanks, for instance. We can't. We have to win by winning, not by hoping someone else will lose. Remember . . . the season isn't over for this team until the last out on the last afternoon. Now go out there . . . and play ball. . . ."

It was the next afternoon that Jim Casey dropped in the offices of the Giants at the Polo

Grounds. Outside the rain poured down in a September deluge made worse by the lack of rain during most of the long, dry summer.

"Hullo there, Jim. How's things?" The caustic Irishman managing the Giants was in an unusually mellow mood. He saw another pennant and a chance for one more crack at his old rivals coming. Offering his visitor a long Havana cigar, he lit one himself, exhaled the smoke, and stared at the ceiling of the office which once had belonged to the illustrious John McGraw.

"Well, Bill, things look pretty good for you fellas."

"Yep, I guess so. We have eight or nine tough games ahead, a doubleheader account of this rain with the Cubs tomorrow, then four with the Bees. Bees are tough now, they've won nine out of fourteen; funny thing, that club's way down, too. Then we can ease up a little, we finish with three games against the Dodgers over here. Well, it's been a tough fight, but so far we haven't felt the strain too much; we been loose and none of the boys have tightened up. Trick now is to stay loose, to be on our toes, to hustle. If we could only forget we were leading the League; but of course that's mighty difficult, especially when you get near the end."

"How about the team? Everyone okay?"

"Yeah, everyone except the pitchers. Honeyman and Kleinert aren't in such good condition. But say, the fellows have been great. Casey, they'll do anything; you know, I don't have to worry about anybody staying out late at night, or breaking training rules, or other things. I've told 'em all they can drink beer, and I'll bet there isn't one who has gone in for the hard stuff. Never saw a bunch co-operate the way these lads have. If we can only stay loose and keep playing the kind of heads-up ball we been playing, it's in the bag."

"Yeah. Well, Bill, you gotta watch the Cubs; they're hot. And maybe the Dodgers too. Looks like they might have snapped out of that slump. Did you notice what they did yesterday to Pittsburgh, 17 to 3? Knocked three Pirates out of the box. Young Tucker came back into the line-up, got three for three. About time they worked themselves from that slump, the Dodgers . . ."

"The Dodgers!" He put his feet on the table opposite the desk, leaned back in his swivel chair, and roared. His laughter was full and hearty.

"The Dodgers! Say—is Brooklyn still in the League?"

22

Usually the dressing room before a game was a noisy spot. Not this time. Usually there were shouts of laughter, loud calls for the Doc or old Chiselbeak. Not this time. Usually there was horseplay and wisecracks too. But not that afternoon. Already, an hour before the game, the team had been obliged to fight their way through a mob outside the gates to reach the locker-room entrance, and the ticket sale had stopped at every box office. So it was a grim and tight-lipped crowd of boys who started getting ready for the last game of all, the game on which the season and the pennant depended.

Everyone attended to the business of dressing with determination and despatch. Now they were sitting round, tying the final shoelace and doing those last-minute things that have to be done before taking the field. A few were glancing carelessly at newspapers, others were nervously chewing gum or staring at the floor, a few were rubbing oil into the pockets of well-oiled gloves. Overhead on three sides of the big room where no one who entered could possibly miss them, Chiselbeak had tacked three large printed signs.

"THE TEAM THAT BEATS BROOKLYN WILL WIN THE PENNANT." It was Murphy's wisecrack when the season opened come back to roost in the visitor's dressing room at the Polo Grounds.

Roy, tense and tightened like the rest, sat on the bench before his locker and tried to read Casey's column in the early edition of the afternoon paper. The words of the chunky sportswriter danced before his eyes, and he found himself obliged to read and reread sentence after sentence to get their meaning.

"Well, lads, you could have knocked me over with a Flatbush trolley yesterday. The Dodgers are on the move again. More than that, they come to the final game of the season in the one place baseball wouldn't expect to find them, half a game behind Murphy's Giants. Don't ask me how they've done it. The team that looked like a joke in fourth place a few weeks ago suddenly snapped out of it and started to function. Nothing could stop them. In succession they whaled the Pirates and then the Cubs, took two out of three from the Cards and in the last two games against the League leaders they've battered four Giant hurlers from one end of the Polo Grounds to the other.

"The Brooklyns are fielding and they're hitting also. Roy Tucker, for instance. Three weeks ago the Connecticut farm boy was just another guy named Joe, and then after going fifteen games without a hit he silenced the fans as he used to, getting a single and two doubles out of three times at bat against the Pirates. Since then he hasn't gone hitless in a single game. The Kid from Tomkinsville is pretty far behind in home runs now, but he's hitting .325 and he's bringing in runs in that second slot. So is Swanson, so is big Babe Stansworth, a pretty reliable man behind the bat.

"The pitchers are all in one piece at last and they are pitching heads-up ball. Dodger pitching all summer has been good; last two weeks it's been sensational. That combination of Street and Davis around second base is just about the best in the League. You think you've got the team in a hole and then one of them comes up with a doubleplay ball that nips a rally and saves another game. This rookie Street is one of the main factors in the Dodgers' sudden rush to the front. You look up to see him behind second on one grounder and somewhere back of third on the next. They ought to put a cowbell on his neck so folks can tell where he is. Honest, the way this ballclub is going now would bring tears to the eyes of a rocking horse."

That wasn't all. But the door banged and everyone jumped. It was Dave followed by MacManus, strangely quiet and calm. Dave had a ball in his hands, slapping it from one fist to the other as the Kid's paper slid to the floor and he rose with the others, ready to go. MacManus stepped forward. Taking off his eyeglasses, he twirled them in his hand. His voice was low.

"Just want to say one thing. I've been in this game ever since I left college and played semipro ball up in northern Michigan, and I never seen a better fight or a finer ballclub than this one. I hope you win today. Gosh, I sure hope you win. I want to see you go in there next week in the Series and trim those Yanks the way you did in the exhibition games last year, and I think you can do it, too. But whether you win or lose this afternoon . . . I'm for you . . . all . . . everyone . . . understand? . . .

"One thing more. The manager of the team we play today doesn't think much of Brooklyn. Maybe you remember the crack he made to Casey the sportswriter several weeks ago when we were in that slump in fourth place. He said . . ." For the first time his voice became vibrant and there was passion in his tone. "He said, 'Is Brooklyn . . . still . . . in the League?'

"Don't forget that crack out on the field today."

There was silence for a few seconds when no one seemed to breathe. Then they turned and went out for the last time, a team that three weeks previously had been in fourth place and now, half a game behind the leaders, was fighting for the pennant.

Clack-clack, clackety-clack, clack-clack their spikes sounded on the concrete runway leading to the field.

The crowd rose with a roar as the first man appeared at the entrance of the runway. There they are, there they are . . . the Dodgers!

Sixty thousand frenzied human beings packed the stands behind the plate, jammed into the upper tier which encircled the playing field, stood up two or three deep in the rear. A sell-out. A sell-out at the Polo Grounds. Not for the Series itself could another person have jammed in. Because sport offers no more inspiring spectacle than the man or the team who comes back, who takes the cracks of fate and pulls together to rise once more. Down-and-out, the Dodgers were on the way back. And the roars of the throng which beat about their ears was proof of the tribute of the fans.

While they spread upon the field, another but a derisive cry arose. It had a jeering, taunting note; it was bitter and it was hostile because it came from the Brooklyn crowd behind third, many of whom had been in line all night. Like a wave it rose, fell, rose again, stomp . . . stomp . . . stomp . . . as the men with GIANTS on their shirts took the diamond.

"IS BROOKLYN . . . STILL . . . IN THE LEAGUE? . . . IS BROOKLYN . . . STILL . . . IN THE LEAGUE? . . ."

. . . .

A roar of sound swept into the quiet and orderly living room on the farm. It was late September and there was a chill in the air, and Grandma was sitting before the radio with a cup of tea in her lap. Tea without milk, too. Tea without milk in the late afternoon always kept her awake, but that redoubtable old lady felt the need of something strong. Tea without milk was the strongest thing she could think of. That roar filled the room, it swelled and grew, as Grandma, the tea in her lap, her face flushed, rocked back and forth.

The telephone rang.

For a moment Grandma sat there, then with decision marched into the other room and, taking the receiver off the hook, set it face down on the table. The jangling of the bell instantly stopped and a voice from the radio came into the room.

". . . yes, folks, and believe me, that one run looks big, awfully big right now . . . and here comes Tucker, 'Bad News Tucker' as the boys call him because he's been breaking up so many ball games with that little old stick of his; just hear those fans give him a hand; yep, even the Giant rooters . . ." And once again the noise echoed across the room in that little Connecticut farmhouse.

"Moe Kleinert looks round the diamond . . . he brings up his leg . . . throws . . . and it's a strike! Strike one against Roy Tucker, men on first and third, one out and the Dodgers leading by a single run in the first half of the fourth inning, and *is* this crowd nuts? Listen to 'em howl. Half of 'em want Tucker to crack it and the other half don't. There it goes . . . there it goes . . . a beautiful single into right . . . Tucker slaps a single into right sending Davis across with run number two." The noise drowned out his voice, the noise beat against the walls of the little room, and the announcer was silent for several seconds.

"Yeah . . . there he comes . . . there comes Manager Murphy in from third . . . yep, Kleinert's going out . . . Moe Kleinert, the Giant pitcher, is knocked out of the box, as the second Dodger run comes over with Tucker's clean single, the fourth this inning. That means two runs on four hits, both runs earned. Men on third and first . . . and . . . one out . . . le's see who's coming in . . . I think it's Delaney . . . no, it's Honeyman, Sam Honeyman, the star lefty of the Giants who won twenty-two games this season. He's taken four and only dropped one to the Dodgers. But those two runs sure do look big right now . . . here goes Kleinert . . . Moe Kleinert going to the showers . . . and Red Allen, the Dodger first baseman, swinging two bats in his hand comes to the plate."

Watching the game from the stands, from the press quarters, or from his own box just back of the Dodger dugout, was impossible. The strain was too much, so MacManus paced up and down in a small office back of the press box, which had been assigned him for the three days of the Series. Every once in a while he stepped through a corridor and into the press coop where he looked down over the heads of the newspapermen at work, onto the field. Onto Razzle hitching his trousers and stuffing in his shirt with that familiar gesture, onto Harry Street dancing around at second, and Roy Tucker nervously fingering his cap in right, at Eddie Davis scooping up dirt with his fingers back of second. At Babe behind the plate, at the outfield shifting a little to the left as Dave from the bench moved them around for each batter. He wanted this game, Mac did, he wanted it as he had never wanted anything in his life before. Mustn't let the boys know and that was one reason for keeping away from the field.

". . . so coming into the eighth, and old Razzle looks kinder tired out there on the mound . . . it's two to one for Brooklyn, two men out, men on first and third, and Muscles Mulligan, the Giant first baseman, at the plate." From his little office MacManus snapped the dials of a small portable radio. He could have sat beside the announcer had he wished, but that would have meant being too close. It was easier like this.

"Here's the pitch . . . low and inside . . . ball ONE. The infield's playing a little to the right . . . here it comes . . . IT'S A HIT . . ." The roar drowned his voice; it came over the radio and it also came through the closed door, telling the stocky freckle-faced man of disaster. He stood in the middle of the room, sweat coming out on his forehead. "Mayerson is coming in with the tying run . . . Ronsek going round second . . . coming into third . . . he's going home . . . he's trying for home . . . he makes it . . . another run and Muscles takes second on the throw-in."

The noise of sixty thousand insane spectators again blanketed the announcer's voice. The Giants were ahead, three to two, and the man alone in the room passed his fingers across his wet forehead. "And there goes old Razzle . . . the crowd's giving him a great hand . . . but Nugent is tired . . . just plain tired . . . Leonard's pitchers haven't had enough rest these last few weeks, they're beginning to feel the strain . . . and here comes a relief pitcher from the bullpen . . . wait a minute . . . I can't see . . . yes, it's Leonard's star, Elmer McCaffrey, in for Razzle Nugent, with the Giants leading three to two, one out and a man on second, the last of the eighth. We now pause for station identification."

Down on the sunbaked field Roy kept repeating those words he had been saying to himself all through the game. Until the last out . . . on the last afternoon of the season. Ever since he'd heard that sentence on the day Dave took a chance and shoved him into the line-up again, the Kid had repeated it. Dave was right, Dave was certainly right. It was the ninth. One man was out and the Dodgers were a run behind. But the season wasn't over until the last out. . . .

Up and down the dugout their voices came as he walked up to the plate.

"Now, Roy old boy, old kid. . . ."

"You can do it, Roy. . . ."

"Save me a rap, Roy. . . ."

Maguire, the Giant catcher, stood watching

and noticed something strange. It looked as if he was whistling. Even through the noise and roar from the stands he heard a distinct whistle. As the Kid came close he heard . . . *Yankee Doodle.* That Dodger rookie must be going nuts!

"Ball one." The welcome words from Stubblebeard behind the bat greeted his ears. He had to get on . . . had to get on . . . had to get on . . .

The next pitch. He took it. Ball two.

But the next was a strike and he stepped back to pick up some dirt and rub it on the moist palms of his hands, whistling as he did so. The catcher looked at him queerly.

"Ball three." Three and one. The cripple. Should he hit? This was the one to hit. What would he do in the pitcher's place—shoot it over, of course. This was the one, the one to hit. . . .

Crack!

He was off, for he felt in that ring a ball that had carry. The roar as he dashed down toward first told him it was safe, and everything he had, every ounce of nerve and sinew, went into his strain for an extra base. Old Cassidy was shouting, urging him on, but as he rounded the bag Muscles crowded him ever so little, gave him just enough of a body-check to jostle him and throw him completely off stride. He stumbled down the basepath, caught himself, and tore for second. Ten feet away he hit the dirt and with a hooked slide went into the bag. The ball was still in the fielder's hands as he rose, and but for Muscles' trick he would have had a good shot at third.

Red Allen came to the plate swinging two bats. Watching, the Kid saw Dave from the dugout

THIS WAS THE ONE TO HIT

give the steal signal with a bunt on the second pitch. Roy had been studying Honeyman all summer with the eyes of a former pitcher. The big left-hander had a peculiar delivery, and whenever he threw a ball to the batter he bent his front knee slightly from the normal position. From his toes, arms outstretched, the Kid concentrated on the man in the box, while the great crowd stood yelling passionately in the stands.

There it was. . . .

Down toward third, as Jerry dropped a slow rolling bunt along the base line. The play he knew would be for the out at first. Then as he dug hard into the dirt, a thought flashed through his mind. Here at last was his chance. Like lightning it came to him, the whole play, and here was the one perfect set-up for the thing he had been working on and waiting for ever since his fight with Muscles. This was the moment to take a chance. He raced round third with Charlie Draper on the coaching lines shouting at him to hold the bag. He was twenty-five feet down the path toward home when Muscles, expecting him as usual to turn and dart back for third, drew his arm to throw. Instead the Kid broke for the plate. Muscles bit completely, fired the ball to third, by which time Roy was almost at the plate. He went over standing up and the score was tied.

23

In her room on the second floor she sat sewing, the door half open. Downstairs the children had the radio on, but she preferred to be alone. Too much was at stake, too much depended on what happened over in the Polo Grounds that afternoon, and she felt she couldn't endure the strain of listening to the slow drama on the air.

"Mother! Mother!" The voice of a little girl at the foot of the stairs drowned for a moment the excited tones of the announcer.

"Mother! Motherrr . . . Daddy's going in!"

Her sewing dropped to the floor and she rushed downstairs as his voice filled the sunny living room.

". . . and Stansworth is standing there shaking his head . . . the fellow's in pain . . . Babe Stansworth got that foul tip right on the end of his throwing thumb . . . yes . . . he's chucked his mitt into the dirt . . . boy, does he hate to leave this ball game . . . yes, he sure hates to leave . . . and here comes the bat boy with Dave Leonard's favorite mask . . . Leonard, the Dodger manager, man who pulled the Brooks into this amazing under-the-wire drive for the pennant, is going in. The thirty-nine-year-old catcher will take Stansworth's place behind the bat. . . . Just hear that roar. . . . Those fans are giving Dave a big hand as he slips the chest protector over his shoulders. . . . He pats Stansworth on the back . . . and now McCaffrey is throwing him a couple of balls, there goes a snap throw to second and a pretty good one too. . . . The veteran Dave Leonard, leading his own team at the end of this stirring contest, going into the thirteenth inning with the score still deadlocked at three-three. The whole field is in shadow now . . . this is Luke Cunningham bringing you the crucial game at the Polo Grounds between the Dodgers and the Giants over the Continental Broadcasting System thanks to the courtesy of Starlight Soap, S-T-A-R-L-I-G-H-T. . . ."

As the inning finished and the Kid trotted in from the field, he realized that Dave was right. He was always right, everlastingly right; Dave knew baseball like no one else. The season wasn't over until the last out on the last afternoon. It was the first of the fourteenth, and Roy, leaning on his bat and watching Swanny fly out to the field, realized again that in baseball the impossible could happen. Dave was right.

When he walked to the plate they rose all over the field cheering. Not for him. Why, only three weeks ago they were razzing him, and the boys in right over at Ebbets Field were booing him between innings. Now they were all for him, on account of that play in the ninth which tied the score, so he tipped his cap as he stepped into the box.

The pitcher went into the crouch. Low and inside for a ball. Another pitch, by his cap, and Stubblebeard behind the plate yelled,

"Ball two!"

Was the pitcher weakening? Outwardly Honeyman looked unruffled, but the Kid knew exactly how he felt and wasn't surprised to see a hand go to his hip in a gesture of fatigue. Here it was . . . he swung and missed a curve, a down and inner.

Two and one. The next was on the inside and in the dirt. He looked at it. Three and one; the cripple. The pitcher's leg went up and the ball came . . .

"Ball four." He slung his bat away and trotted to first while behind third the cry came.

"IS BROOKLYN . . . STILL . . . IN THE LEAGUE? . . . IS . . . BROOKLYN . . . STILL . . . IN THE LEAGUE? . . . IS BROOKLYN . . . STILL . . ."

Red Allen up. Old Cassidy back of first gave him the signal to go down on the second pitch. Muscles made no attempt to crowd him, but he took only a conservative lead until he saw that front knee bend, and then . . .

Crack! He was off as the batter swung, rounding second, tearing for third with everything he had. Reaching third he saw them urging him in, so head down he strained for the plate with the run which might win the game. Past third, closer, nearing home, closer, closer, and then ten feet away he saw the catcher waiting, arms open, so he hit the dirt as the ball plunked into the mitt. His momentum carried him ahead into the catcher's legs with such force that they rolled

THE KID SLID HOME

over and over together in the dust. While the ball fell hopping along the grass.

From the bleachers in center came the roar. It echoed back from the stands behind the dugout, bounced across from right field stands to left, fifty thousand humans concentrated on that play. The Kid was yanked to his feet by Harry Street, slapped on the back by Karl Case, surrounded by the entire team who emerged from the dugout, dancing and cheering with delight. But Dave, who missed nothing, was cool in the midst of the noise and excitement.

"Look at yourself, Roy. Go in and get that fixed quick now."

He glanced down at his trousers. There was a long tear on one side and warm blood was oozing down his leg. He turned for the dugout as Doc Masters rushed up and grabbed his arm.

"Come here, we gotta change those pants. Hurry up."

While Red Allen danced off second and Harry came to the plate, the substitutes leaned around him on the bench and his trousers were pulled off. Doc swabbed iodine over the wound, a long nasty-looking cut on the upper part of his leg. Then slapping a bandage over it, he pasted strips of tape across his thigh. The cut throbbed painfully, but what did that matter? They were ahead. Four to three. They were leading the Giants! A minute later he was walking out to right again for the last half of the fourteenth.

The first batter grounded out to Eddie who came up cleanly and smoothly with the ball as if it were the first out of the opening inning. Only two more men to get! Next came a base on balls.

Like Honeyman, McCaffrey was tiring. The Kid knew the signs and could see weariness in his pitching even from the field. Why not? The pitcher had been in six games in two weeks, been pitching for almost seven innings, his second game in three days. McCaffrey was tiring and Dave realized it too. He walked down the path in that feverish atmosphere as quiet and calm as if he had been calling plays at Clearwater in practice. The two whispered together and Dave went behind the bat.

Crack! On the first ball the batter struck deeply to left. Their heads in their shoulders the two baserunners rounded the bags, while Swanny and Karl hustled after the ball and Harry ran far out behind short. By the time it was back there were men on second and third and only one out. Now Dave's words came back with an ominous significance. The race wasn't over until the last out on the last afternoon of the season.

A roar rose from the stands. McCaffrey was leaving the game.

The big pitcher threw his glove disconsolately into the dirt and walked in while the crowd stood yelling. Dave slapped him on the shoulders and then through cupped hands yelled to the bullpen. Through the din Fat Stuff waddled across the field.

Of all people, Fat Stuff! The Kid suddenly saw baseball as if for the first time. The slow good-natured man whom he had always rather pitied because he had only been used this season as a relief pitcher and was on the way out. All summer he'd been the man they sent for when star pitchers got into trouble. Fat Stuff! Old Fat Stuff, the butt of everyone's jokes, patient, smart, steady, Fat Stuff, of all people! It was Fat Stuff on whom the whole season depended. Now he realized how important a relief pitcher was when crisis came, what a vital cog he was in that machine which is a winning ballclub.

"Foster, No. 6, pitching for McCaffrey, No. 30, for Brooklyn."

It was up to Fat Stuff.

. . . .

Down above the lower meadow the sky darkened. Through the kitchen window Grandma could see flashes of lightning in the sky. She poured herself a cup of tea without milk and took it back to the living room. The shadows were deepening in the September twilight, but still that flood of words came from the radio beside her rocking chair.

". . . friends, right now while Foster is taking his warm-up pitches is a good time to ask you a question. *Would you turn your back on a thousand dollars?* Of course not. And ten other cash prizes of five dollars each. Remember the Starlight soap contest is open to everyone, to all fans who simply tear off the cover of a box of Starlight soap and send in the answer in one sentence. WHY . . . I . . . LIKE STARLIGHT . . . SOAP . . . Because . . ." A terrific peal of thunder startled Grandma. She jumped in her chair.

"That's all, no fancy writing necessary, anyone can do it. Remember, fans, you all have a chance and don't forget the name, spelt S-T-A-R-

L-I-G-H-T soap. Don't turn your back on a thousand dollars. Well, here we go back to this great ball game, four to three for the Dodgers in the last of the fourteenth, Muscles Mulligan at the bat, the tying run on third, and the winning run on second. Just hear the Giant fans give Foster the razoo."

Distinctly the noise came into the living room, fifty thousand pairs of hands together:

Clap-clap, clap-clap, clap-clap, clap-clap.

"And here's the pitch . . . he takes it . . . ball two. Foster can't seem to find the plate." A roar filled the room, a roar that was only louder than the continuous background of sound that had been coming all through the last minutes. "Strike one . . . right . . . down . . . Broadway . . . for a called strike. . . ." Outside the lightning was brighter now and the thunder louder. Grandma looked anxiously round to see if all the windows were closed.

"Mulligan batting from a slight crouch . . . there it goes . . . a high twisting foul behind the plate. . . . Leonard is after it . . . back . . . back . . . almost into the Giant dugout . . . the New York players are scattering in front of the bench . . . he has it . . . HE HAS IT . . . a wonderful catch . . . he turns and snaps to Foster at the plate to prevent McKinnon on third reaching home on the play. That was a wonderful catch, what the boys call a 'dilly.' Yessir, that old-timer is still in there. Two out, and the winning run on second, four to three for the Dodgers in the last of the fourteenth . . . and here comes Manager Murphy of the Giants . . . just hear those Dodger fans back of third there giving him the bird."

The cadence entered Grandma's somber living room.

"IS BROOKLYN . . . STILL . . . IN THE LEAGUE? . . . IS BROOKLYN . . . STILL . . . IN THE LEAGUE? . . . IS BROOKLYN . . . STILL . . ."

"Foster looks round . . . Brooklyn infield playing deep . . . the outfield slightly to the left . . . and deep. . . . Foster trying to protect his one-run lead . . . here's the pitch. . . .

"Strike one! A beauty, right through the middle, and Murphy didn't offer at it." The roar rose higher. "Guess Murphy didn't think he had the nerve . . . here it comes . . . a ball. One and one. Across the letters, too high. One and one, two out, men on third and second, the last of the fourteenth. . . .

"Oh, it's a hit. It's a hit!" He was yelling, screaming almost, but the tumult was so great he could hardly be heard nevertheless, and Grandma leaned over toward the radio. "It's a hit, IT'S A HIT, IT'S A HIT, a long drive, was that tagged . . . and there goes that old ball game. A deep drive to right center . . . wait a minute . . . Tucker going over fast . . . Tucker back . . . back . . . back against the fence . . . he speared it . . . no . . . he crashed into the fence. . . ."

There was a frightful explosion outside and the lights went out, cutting the speaker short.

Rain descended. It poured down against the windows, beat on the roof which Roy had covered with the first money he had earned from baseball. In the Connecticut hills round Tomkinsville the storm struck furiously, and Grandma sat silently in the dark. While in the murky dusk of the Polo Grounds a boy writhed in agony on the green turf of deep right center.

Dusk descended upon a mass of players, on a huge crowd pouring onto the field, on a couple of men carrying an inert form through the mob on a stretcher, and meanwhile up in the press box, where the lights were on, Jim Casey for the fifth time that afternoon pulled a piece of copy paper from his typewriter and tossed it, a crumpled ball, to the floor. Once again he started a new lead.

"I've followed every game, had thrills, watched last minute finishes in every sport, but the contest at the Polo Grounds between the Dodgers and the Giants yesterday left me with sixty thousand other fans limp, beaten, and exhausted. The Daffy Dodgers are certainly unpredictable. You can never tell what they'll do, but you can be sure it won't be the thing you imagined. Paced by a has-been relief pitcher, Foster, with Dave Leonard, who is old enough to be in the Baseball Museum at Cooperstown, behind the bat, this crazy ballclub scrapped, fought, disregarded every rule of the game by running wild on the basepaths, making impossible stops and catches in the field, and finally nosed out the Giants to enter the Series next week by a score of four to three in fourteen innings. Led by their brilliant youngster, 'Bad News Tucker,' they went ahead in the fourth, were caught and passed in the eighth, tied the game on a foolhardy bit of baserunning in the ninth, and finally won it by Tucker's leap into the right field fence to spike Murphy's homer in the last of the fourteenth.

"Right now they don't know the extent of Tucker's injuries and whether or not he'll be able to play for the Dodgers in the World Series next week. Just the same, I wouldn't bet five cents against this cockeyed ballclub when they meet the Yanks . . ."

There was a clap of thunder. Rain descended upon the Polo Grounds.

ABOUT THE AUTHOR

JOHN R. TUNIS is considered the "dean" of the young adult sports novel in this country, and has been the leading writer of such books for over four decades. Particularly in the thirties, forties and fifties, Mr. Tunis turned out novels that were eagerly read and discussed by hundreds of thousands of boys and girls. He started his sports writing career in 1920, and was attached to the sports department of the *New York Evening Post* from 1925 to 1932. Then for three years he was connected with the National Broadcasting Company, covering all major tennis matches in this country and Europe. His entrance into radio happened to coincide with a major event in radio history, for he participated in the first transatlantic sports broadcast, during the Davis Cup match between Allison and Borotra in Paris in July, 1932. He has written for practically every magazine in the U.S. from *College Humor* to the *Atlantic Monthly* to the *Horn Book* and *Foreign Affairs*. His books include *Iron Duke, The Duke Decides, Rookie of the Year, Go, Team, Go, Highpockets, All-American, A City for Lincoln* and *Young Razzle*. Mr. Tunis has published many sports novels called "classics," but none more so than the "Tomkinsville Trilogy," composed of *The Kid from Tomkinsville, World Series* and *The Kid Comes Back*.

REACH ACROSS THE GENERATIONS

With books that explore disenchantment and discovery, failure and conquest, and seek to bridge the gap between adolescence and adulthood.

☐	PHOEBE Patricia Dizenzo	2104	•	$ .95
☐	BONNIE JOE, GO HOME Jeanette Eyerly	2490	•	$1.25
☐	NOBODY WAVED GOODBYE Elizabeth Haggard	2670	•	$1.25
☐	THE UPSTAIRS ROOM Johanna Reiss	2858	•	$1.25
☐	DAVE'S SONG Robert McKay	2893	•	$1.25
☐	I NEVER LOVED YOUR MIND Paul Zindel	7993	•	$ .95
☐	THE FRIENDS Rosa Guy	8541	•	$1.25
☐	OX GOES NORTH John Ney	8658	•	$1.25
☐	WHERE THE RED FERN GROWS Wilson Rawls	8676	•	$1.25
☐	RUN SOFTLY, GO FAST Barbara Wersba	8713	•	$1.25
☐	ELLEN: A SHORT LIFE, LONG REMEMBERED Rose Levit	8729	•	$1.25
☐	SUMMER OF MY GERMAN SOLDIER Bette Greene	10192	•	$1.50
☐	HATTER FOX Marilyn Harris	10320	•	$1.75
☐	THE BELL JAR Sylvia Plath	10370	•	$1.95
☐	IT'S NOT THE END OF THE WORLD Judy Blume	10559	•	$1.25
☐	THE MAN WITHOUT A FACE Isabelle Holland	10757	•	$1.25
☐	I KNOW WHY THE CAGED BIRD SINGS Maya Angelou	10842	•	$1.75
☐	RICHIE Thomas Thompson	11029	•	$1.75
☐	MY DARLING, MY HAMBURGER Paul Zindel	11032	•	$1.50

Buy them at your local bookstore or use this handy coupon for ordering:

Bantam Books, Inc., Dept. EDN, 414 East Golf Road, Des Plaines, Ill. 60016

Please send me the books I have checked above. I am enclosing $________
(please add 35¢ to cover postage and handling). Send check or money order
—no cash or C.O.D.'s please.

Mr/Mrs/Miss______________________________

Address__________________________________

City____________________State/Zip________________

EDN—4/77

Please allow three weeks for delivery. This offer expires 4/78.